"What do you intend to do about it, Eulalia?"

"Give it all back, of course. And we'll leave the cottage."

Fenno's slow smile mocked her. "Yes? And where will you go?"

"I'll find somewhere. I'm not a fool."

"No, but pigheaded in the extreme. Come down off your high horse and use some sense."

"I am not pigheaded."

"No, no, of course not—a slip of the tongue. Let us say rather that you are a strong-minded female who likes her own way."

Dear Reader,

To celebrate a fortieth anniversary, be it for a wedding, birthday or some family event, is something of an achievement. Forty years is a long time but that is what Harlequin has done, bringing romance into the lives of countless readers. And romance is something that everyone needs, even if it is sometimes not openly admitted.

Think what pleasure and comfort there is in curling up with a love story with a happy ending when one is feeling depressed or sad or lonely or just pleasantly lazy—there is nothing to beat it, and I'm sure every reader will agree with me. Romance will never be out of fashion or out of date; that is obvious from Harlequin's success in the field of romance over the years. And I, being a romantic down to the soles of my feet, hope with all my heart that in another forty years' time the eightieth anniversary will be celebrated with even greater success. Indeed, I'm sure that it will.

Betty Neels

Fate Takes a Hand
Betty Neels

Harlequin Books

TORONTO • NEW YORK • LONDON
AMSTERDAM • PARIS • SYDNEY • HAMBURG
STOCKHOLM • ATHENS • TOKYO • MILAN
MADRID • WARSAW • BUDAPEST • AUCKLAND

ISBN 0-373-03454-7

FATE TAKES A HAND

First North American Publication 1997.

Copyright © 1995 by Betty Neels.

CHAPTER ONE

THE little flower shop, squeezed between two elegant boutiques, was empty save for a girl in a cupboard-like space at its back, making up a bouquet. It was a charming bouquet, of rose-buds, forget-me-nots and lilies of the valley, suitable for the littlest bridesmaid for whom it was destined, the last of six which she had been left to fashion while the owner of the shop had gone off on some mission of her own. She was tying a pale pink ribbon around it when the shop door was thrust open and a customer came in. A giant of a man, elegantly dressed, no longer young, and wearing a look of impatient annoyance upon his handsome features.

He came to a stop in the middle of the floral arrangements and said curtly, 'I want a couple of dozen roses sent to this address.'

'Red roses?'

'Certainly not. Yellow—pink, it really doesn't matter.'

He stared at her, and really she was worth being stared at: a big girl with generous curves, short dark curly hair, large grey eyes and a pretty face.

He said abruptly, 'What is your name?'

'Eulalia Warburton,' she replied promptly. 'What is yours?'

He smiled thinly. 'The roses are to be sent to this address.' He handed her a card. 'How much?'

'Fifteen pounds and two pounds for delivery.' She glanced at the card. 'This afternoon—this evening? Tomorrow?'

'This evening, before six o'clock. Make sure that they are fresh...'

She gave him an outraged stare. 'All the flowers in this shop are fresh.'

She took the money and thumped the cash register with some force. Thoroughly put out, she said snappily, 'If you doubt it, have your money back and go somewhere else.'

'Dear, dear.' He spoke with infuriating blandness. 'Are you having a bad day?'

'It was a perfectly good day before you came in,' she told him. A good thing Mrs Pearce wasn't here—she would have been given the sack on the spot. She handed him an ornate little card. 'You will wish to write a message?'

She took it back when he had written on it, handed him his change and bade him a coldly civil good day. She got a grunt in reply.

She watched his broad back disappear up the street and took a look at the card. It was to a Miss Ursula Kendall and, after a careful scrutiny of his scrawled message, she gathered that he was sending his apologies. Well, thought Eulalia, if he was as rude to her as he had been here, a nice piece of jewellery would be more in order.

She finished her bouquet and began to arrange the yellow roses in their Cellophane sheath; somehow pink didn't go well with a name like Ursula.

Mrs Pearce came back presently, approved of the bouquets and, since it was almost time to close, told Eulalia to deliver the roses. 'I know it's out of your way, so take a taxi—the money's in the till.' She bustled around, rearranging this and that. 'You'll have to take the bouquets round in the morning. Half-past nine—another taxi, I suppose—but it's a good order.'

It had been a pleasantly warm June day, but now that the afternoon was slipping into early evening there was a cool breeze. Eulalia donned a navy blue jacket over her navy and cream patterned dress, gathered up the roses and left the shop, taking a breath of air as she waited for a taxi. Even there, in London, from time to time one had a faint whiff of really fresh air.

The roses were to be delivered to an address close to Eaton Square. She paid the driver and mounted the steps to the front door of a Georgian terraced house. The girlfriend, if it was a girlfriend, lived in some style, thought Eulalia, and pressed the bell. The door was flung open at the same moment and a young woman stood frowning at her.

'I'm just going out...'

She was a handsome girl. Her features were too strong to be called pretty but she had beautifully dressed fair hair and large blue eyes, which for the moment held no warmth; moreover, she was dressed in the very height of fashion.

'Miss Kendall?' asked Eulalia sweetly. 'I was asked to deliver these to this address before six o'clock.'

Miss Kendall's perfectly made-up mouth thinned. She snatched the flowers and tore open the little envelope attached to them, glanced at the note and pushed the flowers back into Eulalia's arms. 'Throw them with the rubbish,' she demanded angrily. 'If he thinks he can——' She stopped. 'And don't just stand there—take the beastly things and go!'

'I simply cannot throw them in the bin,' said Eulalia firmly. 'They're fresh and beautiful.'

'Then take them home with you—eat them for your supper for all I care.' Miss Kendall turned suddenly and went into the house and banged the door.

They deserved each other, decided Eulalia, walking briskly to the nearest bus-stop. She hadn't liked her ill-tempered customer; she didn't like Miss Kendall either. A well-matched couple. She dismissed them from her mind and boarded a bus to take her home.

Home was a basement flat in Cromwell Road—not the best end by any means, but it was on the edge of respectability and the flats in the rest of the house were occupied by quiet people. It was dark and poky but it had a narrow strip of garden at the back and she had been lucky to get it. It was a worrying thought that the five-year agreement she had would run out before the autumn, but she had been a good tenant and she hoped that the landlord would renew it and not put the rent up. She tried not to think what she would do if he did that...

She went down the steps and opened the narrow door. The room beyond was fair-sized, with a window at the back as well as the barred one beside the door, and it was nicely furnished with chairs and tables and a heavy sideboard which must have come from a larger house. The curtains were chintz, drawn back from the net-curtained windows, and the floor was covered with a rather fine if shabby Turkish carpet. There were two doors along the inner wall, and one of them opened now to reveal a boy of eight or so, who came through followed by an elderly woman with rosy cheeks and a round face crowned by grey hair strained back into a bun.

Eulalia put down the roses and hugged the boy. 'Hello, Peter, have you had a good day at school? Tell me about it presently. Trottie, dear, I'm sorry I'm a bit late. I had to deliver these but they weren't wanted, so I brought them home.' She laid the roses down on a table, one arm round the boy. 'Did that man come about the leak in the bathroom?'

'That he did, Miss Lally, and a fine mess he left behind him too. Said he'd send the bill. Supper's ready when you are.'

'Two ticks,' said Eulalia, and went through the door to a narrow lobby with three doors. She opened one of them and, with Peter still with her, went into her room. It was very small, with one window, barred like all the others, but there was a colourful spread on the narrow bed, and cushions and a pretty bedside lamp. She hung her jacket in the corner cupboard, peered at her face in the old-fashioned looking-glass and said cheerfully, 'Let's have supper. I'm famished, and Trottie will have something delicious...'

Trottie had laid the table under the back window, and Eulalia went through the second door into the narrow kitchen and helped carry through the toad-in-the-hole and jacket potatoes, while Peter filled their glasses with water. It was a simple meal but eaten off old and beautiful china salvaged from her old home, as were the knives and forks and spoons, rat-tailed eighteenth-century heavy silver. Trottie wrapped them up carefully each evening and put them in a felt bag and hid them under her mattress. The discomfort was worth it, she had observed, for if they should be burgled even the worst of villains would hesitate to get an elderly lady out of her bed. Eulalia wasn't sure about that but she forbore to say so.

She found it a cheerful meal, listening to Peter's comments on his day at school, exchanging gentle gossip with Trottie, telling, with a wealth of detail, of the customer who had bought the yellow roses and how they had been rejected.

'They must have cost a pretty penny,' observed Trottie, and when Eulalia told her she said, 'My goodness gracious, we could eat like fighting cocks for a week on that.'

'What's fighting cocks?' said Peter, which led inevitably to the vexed question as to whether it would be unkind to have a rabbit in a hutch in the garden. They had decided against a dog long since, for there was no one to take him for walks. Eulalia was out all day, Trottie had the house to see to and Peter was at school. Even a cat would be risky, with so much traffic along the busy road.

'As soon as I've made my fortune,' said Eulalia, 'we'll move to a very quiet road with trees and big gardens and we'll have a cat and a dog and a rabbit too.'

'I suppose we couldn't go to the country?' asked Peter wistfully.

A wish she silently echoed. Oh, to be back in her old home in the Cotswold village where she had been born, in the nice old house to which her grandmother had whisked her when her parents had died in a car crash. She had been eight years old then and had spent the rest of her childhood there, and later, when her grandmother had grown frail, she had taken over the housekeeping with Miss Trott's aid. It was only on the old lady's death that she had discovered that the house was mortgaged and that there were debts...

She had paid them off and then, with Miss Trott's staunch company, had set off for London with the small amount of money she had salvaged and the promise of a job in the flower shop run by a sister of one of her grandmother's old friends.

She had laid out most of her money on the flat, its rent low because of the recession, signed a lease for five years and, with her wages and Miss Trott's pension, they had carved a life for themselves. It wasn't much of a life but neither of them complained; they had a roof over their heads and enough to eat. It had been towards the end of the third year that she had had a letter from her grandmother's solicitor. A cousin—one she had never known that she had—and her husband had been killed in a plane disaster, leaving a small boy. There were no members of the family save herself, and was she prepared to give the boy a home?

She had gone to see the solicitor and was assured that the facts set out in his letter had been true; the child, unless she was prepared to give him a home, would have to go to an orphanage. There was a little money, she had been told, enough to send him to prep school and, provided he could win a scholarship, pay for his further education. Of course she had agreed to have him, her kind heart wrung by the thought of the lonely little boy, and she had never regretted it. Between them, she and Trottie had helped him with his grief, found a decent school not too far away from the flat, and turned themselves into a family.

They finished their early supper, discussing quite seriously where it would be nice to live, the puppy they would have, a kitten or two and a rabbit—because of course the garden would be large enough to house all three... It was a kind of game they all played from time to time, Peter firmly of the opinion that one day it would all come true, while Eulalia and Trottie hoped for the best. Miracles did happen, after all.

Eulalia helped Peter with his homework presently, while Trottie cleared away the supper things, and when that was done they read a chapter from *The Wind in the Willows* together before a noisy bath-time in the minute bathroom leading off the kitchen. Peter went to bed, and once he was asleep Eulalia sat down at the table to do her anxious sums and count the money in the house. They managed, the pair of them, to keep their heads above water but there was never any money over. Peter was growing fast, the children's allowance was barely enough to keep him adequately clothed, and as for shoes...

She sat chewing the top of her ballpoint, ways and means for the moment forgotten, while she admired the roses displayed in a vase on the sideboard. Which, naturally enough, led her to think of the man who had bought them. He might, even at that very moment, be with his Ursula, apologising abjectly... No, he wouldn't! she corrected herself. He wouldn't know how to be abject... Then, neither would his Ursula. They would stare coldly at each other, concealing bad tempers in a well-bred manner. 'And good luck to them,' said Eulalia, so loudly that Trottie jumped and dropped a stitch of her knitting.

Eulalia had to explain about the rejected roses when she got to the shop in the morning. 'It was too late to bring them back, and besides, Miss Kendall tore the wrapping.'

'Can't be helped,' observed Mrs Pearce. 'No point in bringing them back—he paid for them, didn't he?' She added, 'Men do such silly things when they're in love.'

Eulalia agreed, although she didn't think that he had behaved like a man in love. Very tight-lipped. He wouldn't do for me, she reflected, preparing to gather up the wedding bouquets and convey them in a taxi.

Her destination was a palatial mansion in Belgravia, the home of the bride and, judging by the coming and going, the wedding was going to be a day to remember. She was admitted at the side door, bidden to wait, and then led through a bleak passage into a kitchen and out again through a baize door to the entrance hall—a gloomy place with a lot of marble about and a very large chandelier hanging from its lofty ceiling. Here the bouquets were taken from her by a vinegar-faced lady in a black dress and borne away up the wide staircase. 'Wait here,' she was told sourly, and since there were no seats she wandered around, studying the large paintings on the walls. They were as gloomy as the hall, depicting scenes of battle, dying ladies in white robes, and dead ducks lying in a most unlikely fashion beside bowls of fruit and bunches of flowers.

'Absolutely awful,' said Eulalia in her clear voice, and turned round to see if there was anything better on the other wall.

The man who had bought the roses was standing at the foot of the staircase watching her. He looked rather splendid, in a morning coat with a carnation in his buttonhole, and she felt an unexpected pang at the thought of him marrying his Ursula, who most certainly didn't love him. He would be hard to love, of course, with that air of knowing best all the time...

She eyed him, her lovely head on one side. 'You look magnificent,' she told him, 'and I dare say you'll be very happy. She's quite beautiful and I dare say you made it up. Well, you'd have to, wouldn't you, since you're getting married...?'

'Your impertinent remarks are wide of the mark, Miss—er. I am not the bridegroom, nor indeed do I find it any of your business.'

He was as cross as two sticks, but she was glad he wasn't getting married. 'So sorry,' she told him cheerfully. 'I brought the bouquets, you know.'

'I did not know, nor am I the least interested. Why are you waiting here?'

'I was told to. By someone in a black dress. She had a sharp nose.'

His thin mouth quivered just a little. 'Then I will leave you to await her return. Good day to you, Miss—er.'

He crossed the hall and disappeared through a doorway and shut the door after him. At the same time the vinegar-faced lady came back, told her that the bouquets were satisfactory and that she might go. 'Through the side door.'

'I expect you're tired, and overworked and cross,' said Eulalia kindly, and nipped back down the bleak passage and out through the side door, to catch a bus and be borne back to the shop.

She was kept busy all day, for Mrs Pearce had built up quite a reputation for the perfection of her floral arrangements and there was a steady stream of customers, carried away by the sight of the flowers displayed so enticingly in the June sunshine. Besides, Eulalia was a very pretty girl and knew just how to please them, waiting patiently while they pondered their choice.

She didn't go home for lunch; the bus cost money, for one thing, and for another, if the shop stayed open during the lunch-hour there was always a sprinkling of office workers, mostly husbands wanting flowers sent to their wives for an anniversary. Eulalia, a romantic girl, took great pains with them.

She worked on Saturdays, too, which meant that Peter, home from school, had to rely on Trottie's company, but they spent their Sundays together, taking picnics to the parks in the summer and visiting museums in the cold weather. It wasn't ideal but it couldn't be helped. Mrs Pearce closed the shop on Mondays, which meant that Eulalia could stay at home and do the washing and ironing and then go to the local shops and stock up with groceries for the week. It worked well enough; since she and Peter spent their Sundays away from the flat, it gave Trottie a day to herself.

Going home that evening in a crowded bus, she planned what they would do at the weekend. They would take a bus, riding on the top, of course, and feed the ducks in St James's Park. Banana sandwiches as well as Marmite, she decided, apples, and she would make some sausage rolls before she went to bed on Saturday. Orange squash, because he liked it, and some chocolate... He was a contented child and wise beyond his years, for he never asked her for something he knew she couldn't afford.

It was a splendid morning as they left the flat on Sunday. It would be warm later, but now, in the comparative quiet of a Sunday morning, it was pleasantly cool. The bus was half-empty, so they had an upstairs front seat. At times, reflected Eulalia, parts of London were delightful. There would be no hardship in living in one of the elegant houses which lined the streets through which the bus lumbered. Peter, as though he had read her thoughts, said, 'I'd like to live here. Do you suppose we could move one day?'

'Just as soon as I make my fortune,' she promised him, 'but that may take a little time!'

'You could marry a very rich man, Aunt Lally.'

'Indeed, I could. Perhaps you will find him for me, dear.'

They were nearing the park, and made their way down to the platform, where they exchanged the time of day with the conductor and got off at the next stop.

There weren't many people about, for it wasn't ten o'clock yet. They wandered along, looking at the bright flowerbeds and presently feeding the ducks, before going to sit down in the sun.

There were plenty of people about now. They wandered on and presently sat down again to eat their lunch, and since Peter wanted to walk and there was plenty of time before they need go back again for tea, they had a last look at the lake and crossed the park to the Mall, crossed into Green Park and turned into Piccadilly, where Eulalia suggested that they might get a bus. However, Peter wanted to walk through the elegant streets with their big houses. 'We can go as far as Park Lane,' he pointed out, 'and catch a bus there.' Nothing loath, she agreed. She seldom had the chance to walk for any distance and, although the streets of London, however elegant, weren't a patch on the country roads in the Cotswolds, it was pleasant enough to walk through them.

'I dare say dukes and duchesses live here,' said Peter. 'Do you suppose they're very grand inside?'

'Certainly—lovely curtains and carpets and chandeliers...' She enlarged upon this interesting subject as they walked, until in one of the quiet streets they came upon a magnificent dark grey Bentley and Peter urged her to stop while he took a good look at it. He circled it slowly, admiring it from all angles.

'I shall have one, when I'm a man,' he told her, and laid a small, rather grubby hand on its bonnet.

'Peter, don't touch. The owner would be very angry if he were to see you doing that.'

She let out a great gusty breath when a quiet voice said in her ear, 'A wise caution, Miss—er. You should exercise more control over your son.'

They had been standing with their backs to the terrace of grand houses. Now she shot round to face someone who was beginning to crop up far too frequently. 'It's you,' she said crossly. 'I might have known.'

'Now, why do you say that?'

'No reason at all. I'm sorry if Peter has annoyed you; he had no intention of doing so.' She moved away and took Peter's hand. 'Apologise to this gentleman, dear. I know you meant no harm but we mustn't forget our manners.'

The boy and the man studied each other. 'I'm sorry,' said Peter finally, 'but it's a super car and I wanted to look at it.'

The man nodded. 'Goodbye, Peter; goodbye Miss—er.'

He watched them go, smiling a little. A pity he couldn't remember her surname, and they were hardly on such good terms that he could address her as Eulalia.

'You look cross, Aunt Lally,' said Peter, as they reached a bus-stop and joined the short queue.

'Not with you, love; that man annoyed me.'

'Was he rich?' Peter wanted to know. 'He must be if he lives in one of those houses and drives a Bentley.'

'I dare say he is, but I really don't know. Here's our bus.'

Peter told Trottie all about it when they got home. 'Aunt Lally was a bit cross with him,' he explained.

At Trottie's enquiring look Eulalia said, 'It was the man who bought the roses,' in a voice which didn't invite questions.

*　　*　　*

A week went by. Eulalia, fashioning bouquets and taking orders for beribboned, Cellophaned flowers to be sent to wives and girlfriends and mothers, longed silently for her old home, with its large untidy gardens and the fields beyond. She hoped that the people who had bought it were taking proper care of it and had left the frogs in the pool at the bottom of the garden in peace. It would have been nice to show them to Peter.

She gave her head a shake. Moaning over what was past and couldn't be helped would do no good. Rather, she must think of ways and means for Peter and Trottie to have a holiday once school was over. Somewhere not too far from London, and cheap. A farm, perhaps...

The fine weather had come to stay, at least for a time, and they planned a trip to the Serpentine on Sunday. Trottie was going to have her dinner with one of her elderly friends and Eulalia saw her off before she and Peter, carrying their picnic lunch, set out.

They had got off the bus and were waiting to cross the road when a bunch of youths on motorbikes raced past. They were in high spirits and the road was almost empty and they were going too fast. The last one of all went out of control, mounted the pavement and knocked Peter down, narrowly missing Eulalia, and tearing away.

Peter lay awkwardly, his head on the kerb, an arm bent awkwardly under him. She knelt down beside him, panic-stricken but fighting to keep sensible.

'Peter—Peter, darling? Can you hear me?' When he didn't answer she felt for his pulse and was relieved to find his heart beating strongly. She took off her cardigan and slid it under his head but she didn't move his arm in case it was broken. Then she stood up as a bus came lumbering along on the other side of the road. She waved and shouted to the driver and he stopped his bus, and the conductor came running across the street.

'He was knocked down,' said Eulalia in a voice which shook just a little. 'I must get him to hospital...'

The conductor was a spruce little man and he looked helpful. 'The bus passes Maude's 'ospital. We'll have him aboard—quicker than waiting for an ambulance or a taxi.'

'Bless you. He's concussed and I think that arm's broken.'

'Leave it to me, miss. You go ahead of me; 'e can lie on yer lap. We'll have 'im right as rain in no time.'

Between them they lifted Peter, and Eulalia lifted the arm gently and laid it across Peter's small chest and then hurried to the bus. There was only a handful of passengers aboard and no one complained at the delay as she got in, received Peter on to her lap and held him close as the bus pulled away. The hospital was indeed only a very short drive and the driver took his bus into the forecourt and down the ramp to Casualty and then got down to help his conductor carry Peter in. Eulalia paused just long enough to apologise to the other passengers for the delay, and ran after them.

They were standing, the two of them, explaining to a nurse as Peter was laid on a trolley. ''Ere she is,' said the conductor. 'She'll give yer the details.'

He and the driver shook hands with her, looking bashful at her thanks. 'Can't keep the passengers waiting,' said the driver. ''Ope the nipper'll be OK.'

'Your names?' asked Eulalia. 'Quickly, for I must go to Peter.'

''E's Dave Brown and I'm John 'Iggins, miss. Glad to 'ave 'elped.'

She kissed them on the cheek in turn and hurried after the trolley.

Peter had his eyes open now and she took his hand in hers. 'Peter? It's all right, love. You fell down, you're in hospital and a doctor will come and see if you're hurt.'

'If you'll give the details to the receptionist,' said the nurse, 'we'll get him comfy and get someone to look at him. An accident, was it?'

Eulalia told her briefly and took herself off to the reception desk, and by the time she got back Peter was on an examination couch. His clothes had been taken off, the sleeve of his injured arm cut to allow the small arm to be exposed. He was trying not to cry and she went and held his good hand, wanting to weep herself.

The young doctor who came in said, 'Hello,' in a cheerful voice, then, 'So what's happened to this young man?'

He was gently examining Peter's head as he spoke. He peered into his eyes, then turned his attention to the arm. 'Can you squeeze my finger, old chap?' he wanted to know, and at Peter's whimper of pain, said, 'I think an X-ray first of all, don't you? So we can see the damage.'

He smiled at Eulalia. 'We'll take care of him. If you'll wait here?'

She went and sat down on a bench, oblivious of her torn dress and dishevelled person. There were few people around: two or three at the other end of Casualty, talking quietly, and near them were curtains drawn round one of the cubicles. The curtains parted presently and a big woman with an air of authority came out, followed by a man in a long white coat. She would have known him anywhere because of his great size, and she watched him go and speak to the group near by with a feeling that she was never going to be rid of him. Hopefully, he'd go away without seeing her...

But he had. He shook hands with the two women, and with the man with them, and trod without haste towards her.

He looked different, somehow, and he *was* different. He was someone in authority, ready to help and capable of doing just that. She stood up to meet him, her skirt in tatters around the hem, dust from the street masking its colour. 'It's Peter, he was knocked down by a motorbike—we were on the pavement. He hit his head and I think his arm is broken. He's been taken to X-Ray. I was told to wait here.'

She was pale with worry and her voice shook and so did her hands, so she put them behind her back in case he should see that and think her a silly woman lacking self-control.

'Where did it happen?'

She told him. 'And those two men on the bus, they were so quick and kind. I don't know what I would have done without them.'

'I suspect that you would have managed. Sit down again. I'll go to X-Ray and see how things are.'

She put a hand on his sleeve. 'Do you work here? I mean, you're a doctor in Casualty?'

'Not in Casualty, but I work here upon occasion. I am a surgeon.' He added, 'Orthopaedics.'

'Bones,' said Eulalia. 'You'll help Peter?'

'It seems that since I'm here I might as well.'

She watched him walk away. He had spoilt everything with that last remark. She had been beginning to like him a little but she had been mistaken; he was a bad-tempered man and rude with it. All the same, she hoped he would do something for Peter. Quite unexpectedly, two tears escaped and ran down her pale cheeks. She brushed them aside impatiently, and just in time as he came back.

'Mild concussion, and he has a fractured arm just above the wrist. We will give him a local anaesthetic, align the bones and put on a plaster. We'll keep him overnight for observation...' And at her questioning look he added, 'No, no, nothing to worry about. Routine only. You can fetch him in the morning, but telephone first. Keep him in bed for a couple of days and no school for a week.'

'He's all right?'

He said impatiently, 'Have I not said so? Come and see him before we put the plaster on.'

He turned on his heel and walked away, and she followed him through a door and into a small room where Peter lay on a table. He grinned when he saw her. 'He said I was brave,' he told her. 'I'm going to stay here tonight. You will fetch me, won't you?'

'Of course, dear.' She glanced around. There was no sign of any doctor, only a male nurse and a student nurse busy with bowls of water and plaster bandages.

'Like to stay?' asked the nurse, and gave her a friendly look.

'May I?'

'No problem.' He turned away and lifted Peter's good arm out of the blanket. 'Here's Mr van Linssen. He'll have you as good as new in no time at all.'

So that was his name. She watched as he slid a needle into Peter's broken arm. He did it unhurriedly and very gently, talking all the time to the boy. 'You're a lot braver than many of the grown-ups,' he told him. 'In a minute or two we're going to straighten your arm—you won't have any pain, but you'll feel us pulling a little. Keep still, won't you?'

Peter nodded. His lip quivered a little but he wasn't going to cry. It was Eulalia who felt like crying. She was sure that Peter couldn't feel any pain but she closed her eyes as Mr van Linssen began to pull steadily while the nurse held the arm firmly.

'You can look now,' he said in a hatefully bland voice, so she did. He was holding the arm while the nurse began to slide on a stockinette sleeve and then start to apply the plaster. It didn't take long and Peter hadn't made a sound.

Mr van Linssen was smoothing the plaster tidily when Sister put her head round the curtains. 'Why, Mr van Linssen, I thought you had left ages ago. You'll be late for that luncheon party.' Her eyes fell on Peter. 'Had a tumble?'

'Knocked down by a motorbike. I'd like him in for the night, Sister. Get a bed, will you? And we'll make him comfortable. He's been a model patient.'

She went away and the nurse started to clear up. Mr van Linssen took off his white coat and the student nurse took it from him gingerly. Rather as though he might bite, thought Eulalia. She got up. 'Thank you very much for your help——' she began.

She was cut short. 'No need, all in the day's work, Miss—er?'

He raised his eyebrows, standing there looking at her.

'Warburton,' she snapped.

He nodded. 'Your son's a nice little chap,' he said, and walked away.

She turned to the nurse. 'I'm Peter's cousin,' she told him. 'I did tell the receptionist—he's an orphan.'

'Makes no odds,' said the nurse, and smiled at her; she was very pretty and she had cheered up his day a bit. 'You were in luck. Mr van Linssen wasn't even on duty—came in to see the relations of a patient who died—had a hip op here and got knocked down late last night. He may be a consultant and a bit high and mighty but I know who I'd like to deal with my bones if I broke them.'

Sister came back then and Peter was borne off to the children's ward, sleepy now but rather proud of his plastered arm. Eulalia saw him into his bed and was told by the ward sister that there was no need to come back with pyjamas and toothbrush. 'He's only here for the night,' she said in a comfortable voice. 'Mind you phone first and we'll have him ready for you.'

Eulalia thanked her, kissed Peter and went out of the Casualty entrance. At the top of the ramp there was a dark grey Bentley and Mr van Linssen was sitting in it. He opened the door as she reached the car.

'Get in. I'll drive you home.'

'No, thank you. There's a bus——'

'Get in, Miss Warburton, and don't pretend that you aren't upset. All mothers are when their small children get hurt. Where do you live?'

She got in without another word after she had told him, and they drove in silence until he stopped before the flat. As she got out she said, 'Thank you, you're very kind. And I'm not Peter's mother, only his cousin.'

CHAPTER TWO

MR VAN LINSSEN had expressed no surprise, only grunted, nodded and driven away, leaving her wondering why on earth she had told him. Luckily she wouldn't have to see him again; she would feel such a fool...

She went indoors and was relieved to see that Trottie wasn't back yet. It would give her time to change her torn dress and tidy herself up and compose herself before telling her old friend what had happened. She made a pot of tea and sat down to drink it, reflecting what a good thing it was that she didn't go to work on Mondays; Mrs Pearce was a kind employer but she expected value for her money. She wasn't over-generous with her wages but she was fair. She was also a businesswoman who would have no compunction in giving Eulalia the sack if business fell off, and if Eulalia were to take too many days off she might look around for someone else. Once Peter was home Trottie would look after him, she thought worriedly. Dear Trottie, always willing and good-tempered, and hating the flat as much as she did.

She got up and began to get tea. The sandwiches were still in her bag—they had better have those...

Trottie came in presently, took one look at Eulalia's face and asked, 'What's happened? Where's Peter? You look like a ghost.'

When she had been told she said, 'Poor little fellow. But don't you worry, Miss Lally, he'll be as right as rain in no time. What luck that you're at home tomorrow, and he'll be no trouble—remember how good he was when he had the measles?' She gave Eulalia a sharp glance. 'Did you have any lunch?' She shook her head. 'I thought not. We'll have a nice tea and you can tell me about that doctor. Fancy meeting him like that, and him a medical man. Like it was meant...'

Before she went to bed that night Eulalia phoned the hospital to be told that Peter was asleep after eating a light supper with gusto. Everything was fine, and would she ring after tomorrow's round at noon? He would have been seen by then and an X-ray taken to make sure that the bones were in the right position.

She couldn't imagine Mr van Linssen making any mistakes about bones—after all, it was his work. A tiresome man, not worth sparing a thought for. All the same, it was difficult not to think about him, since he was all part and parcel of their disastrous day.

She fetched Peter home the next afternoon, and since he was to go straight to bed for another two days she took him in a taxi, a rare treat which delighted him. He was full of his stay in hospital; he had enjoyed it, he told her, the nurses had been fun, and the doctor who had seen him in Casualty had come to see him before he went to sleep, and in the morning the big man who had told him that he was brave had come to see him too. 'He wasn't alone,' explained Peter. 'There was Sister with him and two nurses and another doctor and someone who wrote in a book when he said something. I liked him, Aunt Lally, he's not a bit cross really. He carried a silly little girl all round the ward with him because she was crying.'

'I'm very grateful to him, Peter, and so thankful that you weren't really badly hurt. Did he explain that you have to stay quietly in bed for a few days? Dr Burns will come and see you then, and tell us when you can go back to school.' She put an arm round his small shoulders. 'Here we are, home again, and there's Trottie waiting for us.'

He didn't complain at going to bed but sat up happily enough with a jigsaw puzzle. He hadn't a headache but, all the same, Eulalia wouldn't let him read but read to him instead, and presently he settled down and slept, leaving her free to catch up on the household chores.

She began on a pile of ironing while Trottie rested her elderly feet. 'It's no good,' said Eulalia, 'you'll have to have a holiday. Somewhere that will suit you both. The seaside would be nice, or somewhere in the country—a farm, perhaps...'

'Give over, Miss Lally, where's the money to come from?' said Trottie.

'I'll go to the bank and get an overdraft...'

'And what about you?'

'Me? Oh, I'm fine, Trottie, and anyway, I can never have a holiday at this time of year. We're too busy in the shop. I'll wait until the tourist season is over.'

'You said that last year and you didn't go anywhere.'

'Well, things cropped up, didn't they?'

'You mean gas bills and new trousers for Peter and me having to have new spectacles.'

'Yes, well, we'll see. Now, what shall we eat tomorrow? I'll nip out and shop, if you like. Mrs Pearce won't mind if it's only for ten minutes.'

'How about a nice macaroni cheese? That's light enough for Peter—fish would be the thing, but I don't trust fish on Mondays. Mashed swede with a bit of butter, and I'll cream the potatoes. A little egg custard for afters.'

It was a good thing, reflected Eulalia later that evening, that Peter seemed to be quite well again. She had phoned the doctor and he had promised to look in some time tomorrow.

She went back to work in the morning, leaving Trottie to ask questions of their doctor when he came and get his advice. 'I know it's nothing much,' she said, 'but he had an awful bang on his head.'

Mrs Pearce was sympathetic but she didn't offer to let Eulalia go home early. She said with casual kindness, 'Boys will be boys, won't they?' Just as though it had been Peter's fault, and added, 'Luckily you have Miss Trott to look after him. I'll want you to stay a bit later today—Lady Bearsted is sending her secretary for the flowers for her dinner party some time after six o'clock.'

Because she was worried about Peter the day went slowly. Mrs Pearce went home at five o'clock, leaving Eulalia to lock up once the flowers had been fetched. Six o'clock took twice as long as usual to come, and even then there was no sign of the secretary. She came finally, half an hour later, apologetic and harassed. 'These dinner parties,' she confided to Eulalia, 'they're ghastly. I'm supposed to get these flowers back and arranged on the table and round the rooms before everyone arrives about eight o'clock...'

Eulalia took the flowers out to the waiting taxi, watched it drive away and tore back to get her jacket and lock up. At least the rush hour was almost over and it wouldn't take too long to get home.

All the same, it was well after seven o'clock when she reached the flat, to stop short on the pavement. Drawn up to the kerb was a dark grey Bentley.

A jumble of thoughts chased themselves round her head. Peter had been taken ill and their doctor had rung

the hospital and Mr van Linssen had come to examine
Peter. One heard of delayed collapse after concussion—
Peter might be desperately ill. She flung open the door,
almost tumbling down the steps in her hurry.

Trottie was standing at the table, a teapot in her hand.
She looked up as Eulalia came in. 'You are late, love;
you must be tired, and famished into the bargain.'

'Where's Peter? What's that man's car doing outside?
Why is he here?'

She had spoken a good deal louder than usual and
Peter called from his room.

'Aunt Lally—Mr van Linssen's here—we're playing
draughts...'

Eulalia was feeling as anyone would who had believed
the worst had happened and found that there was nothing
to worry about. She had a wish to burst into tears but
she swallowed them and went to Peter's little room. Most
of it seemed to be taken up by Mr van Linssen's bulk.
'Why are you here?' she wanted to know, and then at
Peter's puzzled look she bent to kiss him and smile.

Mr van Linssen stood up, bending his head to avoid
cracking it on the ceiling. 'I happen to know your
doctor,' he told her smoothly. 'We decided that it would
save time if I were to come and check on Peter's progress, since if he were to come he would still need to inform
me of his findings.'

'Peter's all right?'

'My dear Miss Warburton, if he were not, would we
be playing draughts?'

She glared at him. What a nasty way he had of making
her feel a fool. She was wondering if he would go now
that she was home, and hoped that he would, but
Trottie's voice from the living-room begged them to come
and have a nice cup of tea. 'And I'll give Peter his

supper,' she finished, and appeared a moment later with the tray. 'Go and pour the tea, Miss Lally, I'm sure you could both do with a cup, and the doctor can tell you about Peter, for I can see you're all of a fret.'

Eulalia, aware that Mr van Linssen was looking at her with an air of amusement, frowned and led the way, since there was nothing else she could do. Show him the door, of course, but that would be unthinkable. She should be grateful...

There was one of Trottie's Madeira cakes on the table beside the teapot. She poured the tea, offered the cake and passed him the sugar-bowl.

'You work long hours,' he observed, and bit into the cake.

'I had to wait to deliver some flowers. How is Peter, Mr van Linssen?'

'He is perfectly fit, but before he returns to school I want him to be X-rayed again...' At her look of fright he added, 'No, no, don't panic. I merely want to satisfy myself that the bones are correctly aligned and that there is no misplacement. Let me see—it is Tuesday today. Let him stay at home for the rest of this week. Bring him to the hospital tomorrow at ten o'clock.'

He saw the look on her face. 'No—stupid of me, you would be at your shop. I'll arrange for him to be fetched and brought back here. Trottie could accompany him, perhaps?'

'You're very kind.' She was always telling him that, she thought. 'I'm glad he's quite well. He's such a dear little boy.'

'Yes.'

He passed his cup and she refilled it and passed him the cake. 'Are you having a day off?' she asked politely.

'Er—no.' He thought back over his busy day, which had begun with an emergency operation at four o'clock in the morning and was by no means at an end. 'This is a delicious cake.'

She offered him more. It would spoil his supper or dinner, or whatever he had in the evenings, but he was a large man. He might have missed his tea.

He had missed his lunch too, but he didn't tell her that.

He went presently to say goodbye to Peter and to tell him that he would be going to the hospital in the morning for an X-ray. 'And you can go back to school on Monday.'

'Oh, good. Will you come and see me again?'

'Ah, yes, we still have to finish our game of draughts—I'll see if I can find the time.'

Peter was reluctant to let him go. 'Are you very busy every day?'

'Yes, old chap, but now and again I have a day off.'

'I think perhaps I'll be a surgeon when I grow up.'

'A splendid idea!' They shook hands, and Mr van Linssen shook hands with Trottie too, but when Eulalia took him to the door he bent and kissed her, opened the door and went up the stone steps two at a time without a backward glance.

She banged the door shut. 'He's outrageous,' she said furiously.

'You're a pretty girl, Miss Lally. Men like pretty girls.'

Eulalia ground her splendid teeth.

Mr van Linssen drove himself home. He had enjoyed kissing Eulalia but he wasn't sure why he had done so. She was very pretty—indeed, beautiful when she wasn't looking cross—but he had known and still did know other pretty women and felt no urge to kiss any of them. True, he kissed Ursula from time to time, but always circumspectly, as she was fussy about her make-up being spoiled. Their engagement was a well-conducted affair, with no display of emotion.

He had decided to marry her because she was so suitable to be his wife, and since he was no longer a young man and had decided that there was no ideal woman in the world for him. He had known from the first that Ursula didn't love him; she liked him, was fond of him, and very content to marry him, for he had wealth and position and a certain amount of fame in his profession. They would get on well enough together, although she had revealed a pettishness and desire to have her own way which she had been careful not to let him see before they had become engaged. She had lost her temper once or twice and then apologised very prettily, but they had come near to quarrelling when he had told her that for part of the year they would live in Holland. 'My home is there,' he had pointed out reasonably. 'I have beds in several hospitals. My home is in the country and I think that you would like it.'

She had screamed at him—at the idea of burying herself alive in some miserable little village with no shops and none of her friends. She would go mad. Of course, she would go there with him just to visit, but certainly not for more than a week or so. Perhaps they could take some of her friends with them...

He had given her a long, thoughtful look and had walked out of her mother's house, so angry that he couldn't trust himself to speak, and then later he had sent her the roses...

He left the main road presently and turned into an elegant little street off Cavendish Square. His house was at the end of a short terrace of Regency houses and was a good deal smaller than the others, with only two storeys, but it had the advantages of easy access to the mews behind and a minute garden at the back. He got out of his car, got his bag from the back seat and trod the three steps to his front door.

A thin middle-aged man opened it. He had a long face with an expression of resigned disapproval upon it, and his staid, 'Good evening, sir,' held reproach.

Mr van Linssen clapped him on the shoulder. 'Good evening, Dodge. I'm late—I got delayed.' He started down the elegant little hall towards his study.

'Nothing serious, I hope, sir.'

'I got carried away playing a game of draughts and quite forgot the time.'

Dodge looked astonished. 'Draughts, sir? Would you like dinner served very shortly?'

Mr van Linssen, his hand on the study door, nodded. 'Please.'

Dodge coughed. 'Miss Kendall telephoned shortly after seven o'clock, sir. She asked if you were home. She seemed somewhat agitated, so I took it upon myself to say that you had been detained at the hospital over an urgent case. I was to tell you that she intended to go to the theatre with her friends as arranged.'

'Oh, lord, I forgot.' He glanced at his watch. 'Well, it's too late to do anything about it now. I'll have dinner and phone later this evening.'

Dodge's face didn't alter, his, 'Very good, sir,' was uttered in his usual rather mournful tones, but once in the kitchen he informed Mabel, his cat, that it served that Miss Kendall right, always expecting the master to frivol away his precious free time at the theatre and suchlike, when all he wanted to do was to have a quiet evening with a book or in the company of his own friends.

Dodge shook his head sadly and began to dish up. He was a splendid cook, and with the aid of a daily cleaner ran the little house to perfection. He disliked Mr van Linssen's choice of a bride. He considered her rude and arrogant and spoilt; moreover, despite his mournful manner, he was romantic at heart, and wished for nothing better than a love-match for his master.

Mr van Linssen enjoyed his dinner, finished an article he had been writing for *The Lancet*, made several phone calls to the hospital and then sat back idly in his chair. There was plenty of work for him to get on with on his desk, but he ignored it. He was mulling over his visit to Peter. A nice child, unspoilt too, and happy despite his orphaned state and lack of a father or uncle. Eulalia was doing her best, he had seen that for himself, and Trottie, waxing chatty over a cup of tea, had told him a good deal. Miss Lally was an angel, she had confided, and never had any time to herself. Even on a Monday, when she was free, there was the washing and ironing and shopping.

Mr van Linssen, who had only a vague idea about the running of a household, had nodded sympathetically. 'What she wants is a good husband,' Trottie had said, and had poured more tea.

She was an impetuous girl, he reflected now, outspoken too—not every man would want her for a wife. She was, of course, undeniably pretty. It was a pity that they had got off on the wrong foot, and she had made it obvious that she had no liking for him, although she had thanked him for looking after Peter and meant it.

He shrugged his shoulders, a little irritated at his interest in her, and lifted the phone.

Ursula's voice, high with bad temper, caused him to wince. 'I have had a wretched evening,' she told him, 'making excuses for you, and of course we were a man short for supper afterwards. Fenno, you will have to give up your appointments at all those hospitals—there's no need. You've private patients enough, and think of the private hospitals there are—you could pick and choose and enjoy a social life.'

It was an old argument which he had always brushed aside. Now he said, 'But I don't want to give up my appointments, either here or in Holland, Ursula, nor do I intend to.'

She did some quick thinking. 'Oh, darling, don't be cross. I've had a beastly time—the play was a bore and some fool spilt wine down my dress—it's a ruin. I'll have to go looking for another one, and shopping is so tiring.'

He thought of Eulalia's tired face when she had got home that evening and fought a rising tide of impatience. 'I'm sure you'll find something just as pretty as the frock which is spoilt.'

'I'll find something you will like, darling, be sure of that. Don't let's quarrel about something which isn't in the least important.'

Mr van Linssen controlled his rage with an effort. 'I have to ring off. I'll phone you tomorrow.'

When, hopefully, he would feel more tolerant.

He fetched Peter the next morning, much to that little boy's delight. 'We thought there'd be an ambulance,' explained Trottie. 'Shall I come with him? However will he get back?'

'I'll bring him back, and there's no need for you to come, Miss Trott.'

'There's coffee on the stove if you could find time for a cup, sir.'

Mr van Linssen sat himself down at the kitchen table, accepted the coffee and a slice of cake and remarked carelessly, 'You must find this very different from the Cotswolds.'

'Indeed I do, and so does Miss Lally. Made up her mind to go back there one day she has, bless her, though how she'll manage that, bless me if I know.'

'Perhaps she has prospects of marrying? An old friend—an admirer?'

'Admirers enough,' said Trottie, 'but that's not her way—too proud to accept help. Besides, she's not found the right man yet.' She gave a sniff. 'Besides, he'll have to be a proper man, if you know what I mean, able to take her troubles on to his shoulders. She's not one of these modern young women wanting to be something big in the business world, but she's no doormat, neither——'

She broke off as Peter came into the kitchen, his small face alight with excitement. 'Are we going in your car? Is that why you're here?'

'Indeed it is. Are you ready? We'd better be off or we'll be late.'

Mr van Linssen allowed Peter to chatter away as he drove to the hospital, but presently he asked casually, 'Do you want to go to the Cotswolds too, Peter?'

'Yes, 'cos Aunt Lally does. We shall go one day. She said so—she's going to make her fortune and we'll go to the village where she was a little girl and she's going to open a flower shop there and we'll have a dog and a cat and a rabbit and there will be a garden.'

'You might have to wait a bit, old chap.'

'That's what Aunt Lally says too, but I don't mind. When I'm a man I'll be a doctor like you, and then I can give her the money.'

Mr van Linssen's rather stern face broke into a smile. 'And why not?' he wanted to know.

He parked the car and led Peter to the X-ray department, and, when he had been X-rayed, handed him over to Casualty Sister, who fed him chocolate biscuits and a glass of lemonade until Mr van Linssen came back to say that everything was splendid and that he was to come back and have a fresh plaster put on his arm in three weeks' time. 'You'll have to keep that one for another five or six weeks, Peter, but you can use your arm as much as you like, as long as you keep it in a sling if it feels tired.'

'Aunt Lally will be pleased. I'll tell her.'

'Maybe I'll come along some time and explain it to her. Now we must go back.'

'Are you very busy?' asked Peter, as they went back to the car.

'Not this morning, but this afternoon I'm going to operate.'

'Oh, I'd like to watch you.'

'So you shall, when you are a medical student and I'm grey-haired and elderly.'

Peter laughed at that. 'With a beard and floppy moustache and specs!'

'I do wear spectacles occasionally,' said Mr van Linssen apologetically.

He didn't stay when they reached the flat. 'Everything's just as it should be, Miss Trott,' he said. 'I'll let your doctor know how things are, and I've no doubt he will get in touch with Miss Warburton.' He sounded all at once very like a medical man, kind in a distant manner, but quite impersonal.

*   *   *

When Eulalia got home that evening she listened first of all to Peter's excited account of his visit to the hospital, and then to Trottie. Everything was all right, it seemed, and she was grateful to Mr van Linssen for taking so much trouble. She had no reason to suppose that he would leave any message for her; all the same, she felt a vague disappointment.

The weather turned suddenly wet and chilly, which meant that on Sunday, instead of their usual trip to one or other of the parks, she and Peter took a long bus ride, sitting on the front seat on top, sharing a bag of buns and pointing out everything which took their attention. And on Monday Peter went back to school.

It was halfway through the week when Mr van Linssen walked into the flower shop. Eulalia was alone, for it was the lunch-hour and Mrs Pearce had gone home for a while, leaving her to eat her sandwiches and get on with making bouquets for yet another wedding. She sighed as the doorbell tinkled, hoping it was someone who knew what they wanted and wouldn't keep her for minutes on end while they decided what to do. She put down the roses in her hands and went into the shop.

Mr van Linssen, looming over the floral displays, looked larger than ever and bad-tempered to boot.

Eulalia went delightfully pink, and to cover her sudden shyness said, 'Good afternoon, more yellow roses?'

It annoyed her then that she felt shy; from his forbidding appearance he had no recollection of kissing her, and certainly when he spoke it was quite without warmth, ignoring her remark.

'It is only proper that I should inform you of the result of Peter's X-ray, Miss Warburton, and as I was passing this way it seemed as good an opportunity as any at which to do it.'

'It's all right? Trottie said——'

'It is perfectly satisfactory. He must return for a new plaster in three weeks' time and continue to wear it for a further few weeks. He must use his hand normally. Do not get it wet, of course, and if it aches at all there is no reason why he shouldn't have a sling.'

'Thank you for telling me. I really am most grateful.'

He nodded impatiently. 'Do you not close the shop for your lunch-hour?'

'Heavens, no. Lots of customers come between one and two o'clock.'

'When do you take your lunch-hour?'

'Well, I don't. I mean, I have sandwiches and eat them when there's time.'

'The owner?'

What a lot of questions, thought Eulalia. 'Oh, Mrs Pearce goes home. She has a husband to feed, and she has to see wholesalers and so on—it's convenient to do that over lunch.'

His growl was so fierce that she wondered what she had said to annoy him. A quick-tempered man, no doubt. 'You will be good enough to send some flowers to Miss Kendall. What do you suggest?'

'Well, it depends, doesn't it? If it's just a loving gesture, red roses are for love, aren't they? But if it's by way of saying you are sorry about something, then a mixture of flowers—roses and carnations and some of those lilies there and an orchid or two...'

'Perhaps you will make up a bouquet and have it sent round?'

'A large bouquet? Any particular flowers?'

'No. Make your own choice. I'll write a card.'

She watched him scrawl on the card and put it in its envelope.

'It's a waste of money,' she told him cheerfully. 'Miss Kendall threw the yellow roses at me, you know.'

'Indeed?' He gave her a bland look. 'Don't you have a delivery boy?'

'Good heavens, no, that would be eating the profits.'

'You enjoy your work, Miss Warburton?'

'I like flowers and arranging them.'

'But you do not enjoy living in London and working in this shop?'

It wasn't really a question, just stating a fact, and she wasn't sure how to answer him. 'I'm glad to have a job.' She added with sudden asperity, 'And I can't think what business it is of yours.'

'Upon reflection, nor can I. Good day to you.'

He shut the door gently behind him as he left.

'High-handed,' said Eulalia loudly, 'as well as bad tempered. If I hadn't disliked that Miss Kendall on sight I'd be sorry for her.'

It was almost the end of the following week when Peter rushed to meet her when she got home. 'Aunt Lally, oh, Aunt Lally, something splendid—Mr van Linssen's going to take me round his hospital on Sunday afternoon. He knows I'm going to be a surgeon like him and he said I deserved a treat because I've been a good boy. Do say I can go—he says he'll fetch me in his car and bring me back.'

Eulalia took off her jacket and kicked her shoes from her tired feet.

'Darling, when did he say all this?'

'He stopped here on his way home and he said he was sorry you weren't here but he hoped you'd let me go with him. Two o'clock,' added Peter.

She looked down at the eager little face. He didn't have many treats. His small school-friends had fathers and mothers who took them to fun-fairs and the zoo, and in the summer to the sea for a holiday, but he had never voiced a wish to do that, although she was quite sure that he longed to do the same. She might not like Mr van Linssen, but for some reason or other she trusted him. She said at once, 'Darling, how lovely. Of course you can go, and how kind of Mr van Linssen to ask you. Did you thank him?'

'Yes, of course I did, but I said I'd have to ask you first.'

'Well, I think it's a splendid idea. How are you going to let him know?'

'He said he'd be driving past tomorrow morning and it's Saturday so I'll be here.' He lifted a happy face to her. 'Won't it be fun?' His face clouded. 'Only, what will you do, Aunt Lally? Because Trottie's going to her friend's for dinner...'

Eulalia glanced across to the table, where Trottie was arranging knives and forks and spoons. 'I've so many odd jobs to do—not housework, just nice little jobs like sewing on buttons—and I can read the Sunday papers.'

Trottie's eyes were on her face, and for a moment it seemed as though she would speak, but she only smiled. 'Sounds nice and peaceful to me,' she said finally. 'Dear knows you don't get much time to yourself.'

'You must remember every single thing you see,' said Eulalia, as they sat down to their supper.

* * *

Sunday came with blue skies and bright sunshine, and
the three of them went to church before Trottie went to
catch her bus. 'There's everything ready for your dinner,'
she told them. 'Be sure and have it early so's not to keep
Mr van Linssen waiting. I'll be back around seven
o'clock, same as usual.'

It was a nice dinner but Peter was too excited to eat
much. He was ready and waiting for a long time before
two o'clock. 'Perhaps he won't come,' he said, for the
tenth time.

'He said two o'clock, dear, so don't worry—there's
still ten minutes left.'

He came five minutes later and she went to open the
door to him.

Her, 'Good afternoon, Mr van Linssen,' was coolly
polite. 'This is very kind of you.'

He stood looking at her. 'A pleasure. It has struck me
that it might be sensible if you were to come too.' At
her frown, he added, 'There is always the small chance
that I might be called away urgently and Peter cannot
be left alone. Do you dislike the idea very much?'

Upon reflection, she didn't dislike the idea at all. 'I
don't want to spoil Peter's afternoon.'

'Don't worry, we'll leave you somewhere in safe
hands.'

A remark which ruffled her feelings. She was on the
point of making a suitably telling reply when Peter joined
them. 'Are we ready? What a pity you can't come with
us, Aunt Lally.'

'She is coming,' said Mr van Linssen, and shut the
door.

'Do go and fetch whatever you need to fetch. Peter
and I will plan our route round the hospital—you can
have five minutes.'

Her eyes sparkled with temper. 'I don't——' she began with dignity. She caught his eye then. It was very compelling. She mumbled, 'All right, I won't be long.'

Thank heaven she hadn't changed out of the dress she had worn to church; she had intended to get into an old cotton dress and turn out a few cupboards. She brushed her hair, powdered her nose, added some more lipstick, found her bag and went back to the living-room. The pair of them were crouched over a large sheet of paper spread out on the table. A plan of the hospital, she supposed.

'Won't anyone mind?' she asked, as she got into the back of the car. 'Us walking round?'

'Not if you are with me,' he told her gravely.

They went to Casualty first, for once almost empty, and then to the outpatients' hall, before taking the lift to the first floor to inspect each ward in turn, and in each one he introduced them to the ward sister. 'Friends of mine,' he explained, which she found rather high-handed of him. She hardly knew him, and what conversation they had engaged in had hardly been of a friendly nature.

When they reached the theatre block she was left with Theatre Sister in her office and given a cup of tea while Peter, speechless with excitement, was taken to see one of the operating theatres. They were gone a long time, and when they got back Mr van Linssen had a cup of tea too, and Peter a glass of lemonade. Somehow Eulalia hadn't thought of the operating theatre allied to cups of tea. Sister's office was quite cosy, too, and she was young and pretty and obviously Mr van Linssen's slave.

She was one of the junior sisters, she had confided to Eulalia. The theatre superintendent, an awesome lady who ruled the theatres with a rod of iron, only scrubbed for major surgery and always for Mr van Linssen. 'There are two other sisters, but we aren't allowed to scrub for him, more's the pity. He's quite a dish, isn't he? Going to get married soon—he never talks about it, though.'

They went unhurriedly back through the hospital and into Casualty once more, where Mr van Linssen explained with patience exactly what happened to a patient when he arrived, answering Peter's endless questions with apparent tirelessness.

They got back into the car presently and he said casually, 'I hope you will both come and have tea with me. I'm sure Peter hasn't finished with his questions...?'

'Tea?' asked Peter. 'Oh, please.' He turned to look at Eulalia. 'Aunt Lally, can we go?'

It was impossible to refuse without being rude and spoiling the day for Peter. 'That would be nice,' she said pleasantly, and caught him looking at her in his side mirror.

She had supposed that they would go to one of the cafés in any of the parks, but instead he kept to the streets, their surroundings becoming more elegant with every minute. When he stopped before his house and got out and opened her door, she got out too, and stood looking at his house.

'You live here?' she asked.

'Yes. Very convenient for my work.' He went off to help Peter out, locked the doors and ushered them across the pavement and in through the door being held open by Dodge.

'I've brought some friends for tea, Dodge, if you would let us have it shortly.'

Peter held out his hand. 'How do you do, Mr Dodge? I'm Peter.'

Dodge shook his hand carefully. 'How do you do, Peter? I see you've been in the wars.'

'Miss Warburton and her cousin Peter, Dodge.' And Mr van Linssen smiled a little as Eulalia shook hands too.

CHAPTER THREE

EULALIA gave a small sigh as she went into the drawing-room. It was a long room, taking up the whole of one side of the little house, with a bay window at its front and doors opening on to the little garden at the back. It was furnished very much to her taste, with comfortable chairs, an enormous sofa before the hearth, splendid rugs on the polished wood floor, and mulberry silk curtains blending nicely with the chair-covers. There were little lamp-tables too, arranged just where they were needed, and a handsome bureau cabinet in marquetry. She knew a little about good furniture; this she thought was probably a William and Mary piece. It went very well with the cabinet of walnut with floral marquetry on the other side of the hearth, which was of the same period. She might not see eye to eye with her host, but she had to admit that he had excellent taste in furniture.

The doors to the garden were open and Peter had gone at once to look at it. 'Have a look round, Peter,' invited Mr van Linssen, and to Eulalia, 'Please sit down—tea will be here in a few moments. I hope we haven't spoilt your afternoon.'

She sat. 'No, I enjoyed it. It was very kind of you to give Peter a treat.'

'You have his sole charge?' he asked idly. 'Guardian to a small boy is no easy matter.'

'There wasn't anyone else,' she said simply. 'At least, the solicitor couldn't trace anyone from his father's family, and my cousin was an only child whose parents had died. I didn't even know her. Peter's a dear little boy. Trottie and I often wonder how we lived without him.'

'He's hell-bent on living in the country...'

'I know, and we will one day. I don't know how, but we will. Do you like the country, Mr van Linssen?'

'Yes—it's an entirely different way of living, isn't it?'

He talked on, putting her at her ease, slipping in a question here and there, and she, lulled by his quiet friendliness, answered readily.

Dodge came in presently and spread a magnificent tea on the table by the doors. 'The young gentleman will be more at ease sitting at the table,' he explained, and went away to fetch the teapot.

Peter came in from the garden. 'There's a cat in the garden, sitting on a chair,' he told them breathlessly. 'I stroked him and he purred. Aunt Lally, couldn't we have a cat?'

'That will be Mabel, Dodge's cat,' said Mr van Linssen. 'I expect it wouldn't be quite safe to have a cat at Cromwell Road, Peter—all that traffic rushing to and fro. I should wait until you get to the country.'

Eulalia frowned. Talking so much about the country wasn't much help. That she was determined to get there one day was a fact, but he made it sound as though it was a certainty in the not so distant future.

Peter nodded cheerfully and applied himself to his tea. Dodge, despite his sombre appearance, had a warm heart; there were sandwiches, strips of hot buttered toast, buttered scones, chocolate biscuits and a fruit-cake. Peter worked his way steadily through them all, and Eulalia, since she was hungry, saw no point in being lacking in appetite. There was a good deal of her to nourish, after all. Mr van Linssen, long ago resigned to his Ursula's finicky ways and professed inability to eat any but the choicest of foods, derived a good deal of amused pleasure from her unselfconscious enjoyment.

He was an excellent host, although he had no great love for social occasions; he talked of this and that, drank several cups of tea and ate a scone he didn't want, and had to admit to himself that he was enjoying his afternoon. He had refused an invitation to go with Ursula to friends in the country for the weekend, pleading pressure of work. Well, he had had a busy week, and to spend his free Sunday, before beginning on an even busier one, in the company of Ursula's friends with whom he had little in common, would have given him little pleasure.

They were still sitting round the table while Peter ate the last chocolate biscuit, when the doorknocker was thumped, and a moment later Dodge opened the door, to be thrust aside by Miss Kendall.

'Darling, how naughty of you, I do believe——' She stopped. 'What on earth is she doing here? It's the girl from the flower shop, isn't it? And that boy.' Her charming smile turned to tight-lipped offence. 'I came back early, thinking you might like to spend the evening with me, but I can see it's not necessary.'

She turned her back on Eulalia and Peter. 'You said you were going to be busy over the weekend.' She tossed her head and added spitefully, 'With this shop girl, I suppose.'

Mr van Linssen had risen to his feet, listening impassively to this outburst. 'My dear Ursula, shall we overlook this little outburst?' His voice was quiet and cool. 'This is Miss Warburton, who works in the flower shop as you already know, and this is her cousin Peter.

We have spent an hour or so at the hospital, a reward for his pluck when he broke his arm recently.'

Peter had left his chair too and had come to stand by him, and now he held out a small hand. 'How do you do?' he said, mindful of Eulalia's teaching of good manners.

Miss Kendall ignored the hand, and after a moment Peter let it fall and turned a puzzled look on Eulalia. She sat, outwardly serene, inwardly seething, waiting to see what would happen next.

Mr van Linssen, apparently untroubled by his fiancée's ill humour, put an arm around Peter's bony shoulders, for he had seen the boy's lip tremble. He said now, 'I don't know when I have had such a delightful afternoon, Peter. We must do it again some time.'

Oh, no, we won't, reflected Eulalia, and caught his eye. He smiled at her, knowing exactly what she was thinking, and she frowned at him. 'We have indeed had a lovely time, Mr van Linssen, but I think we should be getting home now.'

'Of course.' He turned to Ursula, sulking in a chair. 'Coming with us, Ursula?'

'Whatever for? I'll wait here, and when you get back you can take me out for a meal. I've had a very boring weekend.'

'Just as you like.' He watched as Eulalia and Peter wished her goodbye, only to be ignored, and then ushered them out to the car while Dodge stood at the street door. They wished him goodbye too, and Eulalia said, 'It was a lovely tea,' and smiled at him very sweetly.

'A pleasure, miss, and a joy to see the young gentleman enjoying it.'

No one spoke as they drove away until Peter observed, 'I like Mr Dodge—he looks sad, but he isn't, is he?'

Mr van Linssen laughed. 'Not in the least. I believe him to be quite happy inside.'

'Oh, good. Why was that lady cross?'

'Hush, Peter,' said Eulalia, in what he called her 'aunt' voice, so he hushed.

At the flat Mr van Linssen got out, opened her door and helped her out and did the same for Peter, and then stood looking down at her while she started on her thank-you speech. She had barely begun it when he said, 'Shall we go inside and see if Miss Trott is back?'

She stopped in mid-sentence. 'Come inside? You want to come inside?'

'Shall I not be welcome?'

'Of course you are welcome, and do come in, only I thought—I thought you'd want to get back home quickly.'

He didn't answer but followed her down the steps, took the key from her and opened the door. Peter skipped ahead of them to hug Trottie and gabble the excitements of the afternoon to her. She kissed his happy face and said, 'Darling, how very nice. You shall tell me all about it presently, but here's Mr van Linssen... Can we offer you tea? And how nice to see you again,' added Trottie in her soft country voice.

She offered a hand and he took it and bent to kiss her cheek as well.

'We have just had tea, Miss Trott, at my house.' He glanced at Eulalia. 'I, for one, have enjoyed a most pleasant afternoon.'

'But the lady was cross,' said Peter, and was immediately hushed by Eulalia.

Trottie saw the look on her face and launched into an account of her own day. 'And such lovely weather—you can't beat our English summers.'

'But, Trottie, it rains a lot——'

'Of course it does, things have to grow, don't they? You're a foreign gentleman, sir, what do you think of our weather?'

'Delightful, on the whole. Holland is flat and there is always a wind, and it can be very cold in winter.'

Without quite knowing how it had happened, Eulalia discovered that they were all sitting round the table, and there they stayed for the next half-hour, while Mr van Linssen led Trottie on to talk about her younger days until he said reluctantly, 'I must go back home, I'm afraid, and I dare say it's Peter's bedtime.'

He made his farewells briskly and this time he didn't kiss Eulalia.

When he had gone Trottie said, 'Well, that was a nice little visit to end the day, wasn't it? I'll start the supper, Miss Lally, while you get Peter bathed and ready for bed. I dare say he could eat something in his dressing-gown, for once.'

It was over supper that Peter, warm from his bath and wrapped in his dressing-gown, brought up the subject of Miss Kendall again.

'Why was she so cross?' he wanted to know.

'Well, dear, I think she was surprised to find us there. You see, she wanted Mr van Linssen to take her out and I dare say we spoilt her evening.'

'She was rude,' he persisted. 'She didn't shake my hand, and if she's going to marry Mr van Linssen why didn't she kiss him?'

'I expect she'll do that when he gets home. Now, eat your supper, darling, and then off to bed. School in the morning, remember.'

Later that evening, Trottie said, 'That Miss Kendall doesn't seem the right kind of wife for dear Mr van Linssen. Such a good man. He needs a loving wife, not a woman with a nasty temper and no manners.'

'I dare say she's quite different when she's with him, Trottie.'

'You may depend upon that; that's how she caught him in the first place.' She nodded her elderly head. 'Depend upon it too that she doesn't care twopence for him. Smart, is she, as well as pretty?'

Eulalia thought back. 'Yes—very smart—lovely clothes, Trottie, and perfect make-up. Let's be honest, she's the kind of a wife a man in his position needs—you know, dinner parties and so on.'

Trottie gave her a sharp look over her spectacles. 'If that's what you think a man needs in a wife, then you're much mistaken, Miss Lally.'

'Anyway,' said Eulalia defiantly, 'he has a bad temper and he can be very rude. I dare say they'll get on very well together.'

'You don't like him,' said Trottie flatly.

'I don't know him well enough to have an opinion about him,' said Eulalia which, although not quite true, put an end to the conversation.

She took Peter to school in the morning and then went back to do the chores which Trottie was beginning to find tiring and, those done, she fetched her basket and went shopping, laying out the housekeeping money in a prudent fashion, and all the while her thoughts, which

should have been centred on groceries, kept straying to
Mr van Linssen.

She didn't like him, of course, but she had to admit
that he had been very kind to Peter. He had a nasty
temper, all the same, and she didn't think that his Ursula
would improve that—a very unpleasant young woman
and, as she had reminded herself so often, deserving of
him and he of her.

She went back and had her lunch with Trottie and
embarked on the ironing. There were never enough hours
in a Monday.

It was ten days later when he came into the shop once
more. Eulalia, on her own as it was lunchtime, was sitting
on a stool at the back of the shop, eating her lunch out
of a paper bag: cheese sandwiches and an apple, and a
mug of tea which Mrs Pearce allowed her to brew.

She put the sandwich, half eaten, back in the bag, and
in a voice thickened by bread and cheese, wished him
good afternoon.

'More flowers?' she wanted to know. 'You must be a
very quarrelsome man.'

'What an impertinent girl you are! I never seek a
quarrel, and I might point out that it is no concern of
yours if I choose to quarrel.'

'True. Is it to be red roses this time?'

It gave her quite a jolt when he said yes. So he did
love Ursula, after all. She felt an unexpected pang of
regret. 'A dozen? Two dozen?'

'Two dozen. Send them by Interflora to this address.'

He gave her a card with the address—it was somewhere in Holland—and she wrote it down in the order-
book and asked, 'Is this place a town? Will there be an
Interflora shop there?'

'No, Leiden is the nearest place.'

'I can look it up in our international directory. We get a good many of our roses from Aalsmeer, they'll be beautifully fresh. Do you want to send a message with them?'

Pen poised over the form she was filling in, she waited.

'Yes—happy birthday, and sign it "Fenno".'

'That's an unusual name,' observed Eulalia, busy writing.

'So is Eulalia.'

'Yes, well—this will cost you a pretty penny.'

'That, again, is no concern of yours.'

She raised large grey eyes to him, allowing the lashes full play. 'We make it a custom to mention the cost before the customer pays—just in case they can't afford it!' She gave him a kind smile and a motherly nod of the head, and saw his mouth set like a rat-trap. Why, she wondered, did she feel the need to annoy him when they met? Why didn't she treat him with a cool indifference and be polite? If Mrs Pearce heard her she would be given a week's notice for cheeking a customer.

She began to work out the cost, doing most of it on her fingers.

'Do you not use a calculator?' he wanted to know impatiently. 'I cannot stand here all day while you add and subtract like a schoolchild.'

'I never was any good at maths, and please don't interrupt me or I'll have to start all over again.'

'I'm surprised that you keep your job.'

'Well, you see, Mrs Pearce always takes Interflora orders, only she's not here.' She added her sums and told him the total and dealt with his credit card. 'I'll see that it gets phoned through today,' she told him. 'Does it matter if it's delivered morning or afternoon?'

'Morning.' He turned to go and at the door paused. 'How is Peter?'

'Very well. His plaster is covered with his friends' names and rude messages. We had a note from the hospital to say that he must go there to have a new plaster tomorrow.'

'That is convenient for you?'

She looked her surprise. 'Well, no, but nothing's convenient, if you see what I mean, not when I'm here all day, but Trottie will take him and bring him back.'

'I'll fetch him and take him home again. He'll be going to Outpatients?'

'Yes, but we can't impose on your kindness again. Trottie will——'

He cut her short. 'I have said that I will take him and bring him home—I shall be taking Outpatients' orthopaedic clinic.' He opened the door, wished her a curt goodbye over his shoulder and went into the street.

When she got home that evening she told Trottie and Peter what Mr van Linssen had arranged.

'There,' said Trottie. 'Didn't I know what a good man he is—so thoughtful of others, knowing as how you weren't free to take Peter yourself?'

'Oh, magnificent,' said Peter, who was forever trying out long words. 'Perhaps he'll have time for a game of draughts when he brings me home.'

'Not very likely,' said Eulalia sharply. 'He has to work like anyone else.' Which remark earned her surprised looks from her companions.

Mr van Linssen, driving back to the hospital, told himself that it was interest in Peter which had driven him to offer to take him back to Outpatients in the morning. Certainly it was not his intention to please Eulalia: a tiresome girl and far too outspoken. She needed a firm hand and she wasn't likely to get it, for it would be hard to find a man prepared to put up with her ways. Of course, he conceded, she was devoted to the boy and very protective of Miss Trott, hard-working too, and not easily discouraged. She deserved some sympathy, although she would probably throw it back in the face of anyone offering it.

He parked the car and stalked into his clinic where, contrary to his custom, he snapped the heads off his two housemen, a handful of students and an unfortunate nurse who dropped a pile of notes on the floor.

His clinic lasted longer than usual and his temper, although once more in control, was no better. When he remembered that he was taking Ursula to the opera that evening it grew decidedly worse. To go home and change into a dinner-jacket, go without his dinner and spend the evening being sociable to her many friends, have supper with them afterwards and get home too late to work at the series of lectures he was to give was more than he could tolerate, although he saw no help for it. For once, however, Fate was to treat him kindly, even if she hadn't been as kind to the elderly man knocked down in the street outside the hospital and rushed inside. He was preparing to leave Sister's office, where he had been discussing his list for the following afternoon, when the phone went and he was asked if he would go to Casualty. Theatre Sister was surprised at the cheerful manner with which he responded.

The man was severely injured: a fractured pelvis, fractures of one leg and an arm. Mr van Linssen forgot all about Ursula and the opera and spent several hours in Theatre, putting the bones together again. It was late when he left to go home to Dodge and the kind of meal only Dodge could conjure up at a moment's notice. He was sitting at the table, finishing his coffee, when Dodge told him that Miss Kendall had telephoned twice and he had informed her that his master was delayed at the hospital. He didn't add that she had carried on something shocking, but said smoothly that she had seemed a little upset.

'I'll ring her presently.' He glanced at his watch. 'No, it's too late now. I'll have to do it tomorrow when I've finished the clinic.'

Peter was waiting for him when he drove to the flat in the morning. 'I knew you'd come,' he said happily. 'Grown-ups don't always do what they say they're going to, but you do, don't you?'

'As far as possible, old chap. Jump in or we shall be late.' He bade Trottie goodbye and settled the boy beside him and, once at the hospital, handed him over to the young doctor who had first seen him. 'Give me a ring when you're ready. I'll be in Theatre for half an hour, then in Outpatients.'

It was rather more than half an hour by the time Peter was dealt with, and a nurse was detailed to take him over to Outpatients. Here he was sat on a bench and told to wait until Mr van Linssen came for him, something he was delighted to do, for there was so much to see— patients going in and out, nurses, doctors, porters wheeling trolleys and, best of all, presently Mr van Linssen himself in a long white coat, surrounded by the registrar, his housemen, several students and Sister. He looked, thought Peter, like one of the men in his book of heroes. His small chest swelled with pride because they were friends.

Mr van Linssen lifted a hand in greeting and disappeared through another door, and after ten minutes or so came out again, this time without his white coat.

'Trottie said she'd have coffee ready,' said Peter hopefully in the car.

'Just what I need, but I can only stay for five minutes. I'm operating this afternoon and I must go round the ward first.'

'Yes, of course,' agreed Peter solemnly. 'I'm sure Trottie will understand.'

Mr van Linssen, nicely filled with coffee and a slice of Trottie's cake, went back to work. He had quite forgotten Ursula.

She phoned that evening soon after he got home and he listened patiently to her cross voice telling him just what she thought of him and, since he felt guilty, he apologised handsomely. It was after he had put the receiver down that it occurred to him that he would have to send more flowers...

Eulalia had just opened the shop when he got there the next morning. At the sight of him she said, 'Peter's all right—Trottie said so.' She eyed him anxiously. 'Is something wrong?'

He gave her a pointed good morning. 'Of course not. How you do fly into a panic at the sight of me—am I such a harbinger of bad news?'

'Each time I see you I think it will be the last,' she declared. 'Not more flowers? Hadn't it better be a diamond brooch from Cartier?'

He gave her a level look. 'Do not provoke me. I have a nasty temper, and don't be impertinent!'

He came a little further into the shop and she saw how tired he was. She said, 'I'm sorry, it's my tongue, it runs away with me. I do try to think before I speak but I don't always remember.' She smiled at him. 'You're tired and that makes you cross. You should have a holiday, away from the hospital and London.'

'And my patients?' He was amused and all of a sudden brisk. 'Now, these flowers—something rather special this time, I think.'

Lucky Ursula, reflected Eulalia. She only hoped the wretched girl realised it. It seemed unlikely, but perhaps she really did love him in her way, and she thought he must love her. 'How about pale mauve orchids and fern in one of these vases? They're a bit expensive because they're nineteenth-century Staffordshire—Mrs Pearce goes around the antique shops and buys up the real thing when she can find it.' She held it up for his inspection. 'I'm sure Miss Kendall would love it...'

He said without much interest, 'Very well, send it to her home, will you—some time today?' He paid her, and with a brief goodbye left the shop. She watched him cross the street and get into his car and drive away. Perhaps this really was the last time she would see him...

He hadn't written a card. His car had disappeared into the stream of traffic and there was nothing to do about it. She told Mrs Pearce when she arrived, and was told to write a card herself and take the flowers in her lunch-hour. 'I'll stay here until you get back,' said Mrs Pearce. 'You can go more easily than usual—there'll be plenty of buses around noon.'

It was nice to be away from the shop, even if it was her lunch-hour. Eulalia rang the bell of Ursula's home and a severe woman in a black dress and apron opened the door.

'Flowers for Miss Kendall,' said Eulalia.

She was about to hand them over when she heard Ursula's voice call out, 'Who is it?' and she came into the hall. She eyed Eulalia with dislike. 'You again. More flowers.' She turned to the woman. 'All right, you can go, Mrs Parkes. Hasn't he got more sense than to send flowers? Good God, I get flowers from everyone.' Her eyes narrowed. 'Perhaps he likes to go to your shop and talk to you—is that it? After him, are you? I know your kind, on the look-out for a rich husband, although probably you wouldn't mind if he wasn't your husband.' She sniggered.

Eulalia went pale with rage. 'Here are your flowers. You are a very vulgar woman and spiteful...'

She had thrust the carefully wrapped vase and flowers at Ursula, who took them and then deliberately dropped them on the ground, lifted up a foot and stamped on the orchids.

'They're only flowers,' said Eulalia slowly. 'They never did you any harm and they were beautiful—so was the vase.'

'You haven't heard the last of this,' declared Ursula, and went indoors and banged the door shut.

Eulalia, shaking with rage, told Mrs Pearce when she got back to the shop.

'Oh, dear, they're good customers too, and we were to do the wedding-flowers. You'd better apologise, Eulalia—the customer's always right, you know.'

Eulalia stared at her. 'Mrs Pearce, she was unforgivably rude to me. I didn't start it, you know.'

Mrs Pearce shrugged her shoulders. 'Apologise, all the same, Eulalia—she could lose me a lot of custom, telling tales to her friends; she knows a great many people, you know.'

Eulalia said steadily, 'I'm sorry, Mrs Pearce,' and went to serve a customer.

She told Trottie when she got home that evening, after Peter was in bed and asleep. 'Mrs Pearce was annoyed because I wouldn't apologise, but Trottie, what would I apologise for, and how dare that woman say things like that? She made me feel cheap...'

'A very nasty person,' Trottie allowed, 'and don't you say you're sorry, Miss Lally, whatever happens.'

'Whatever' did happen; Eulalia was given a week's notice when she got to work next Tuesday. 'I'm sorry to lose you, Eulalia,' said Mrs Pearce, 'but I can't afford to lose any business. I'll give you a good reference and you'll get another job easily enough, I dare say.' She paused. 'You won't reconsider apologising?'

'No, Mrs Pearce. Miss Kendall was rude and abusive; she is the one who should apologise. Unfortunately she has money and influence on her side, hasn't she?'

Mrs Pearce looked uncomfortable. 'If you could overlook it...' she began, but seeing the stubborn look on Eulalia's face said no more.

Trottie took the news with a solid calm. 'You did right, Miss Lally, and don't you go regretting it. We've had hard times before, and got through them, and you'll get a job in no time. What have we got in the bank?'

They spent the evening doing sums, plotting and planning. Peter's school fees were safe, tied up in a trust, even if she had wanted to get at them—which she most definitely didn't. It was a question of cutting down on their already tight budget until she found work.

There was little chance to go job-hunting during that week, and she couldn't bring herself to ask for time off to try for any of the likely jobs advertised. She went home on Saturday evening, her last pay-packet in her

purse, feeling scared and defiant at the same time. As
Trottie had said, they had weathered worse storms...

She hadn't told Peter and she didn't intend to until
she had found other work. She spent the next week applying for any likely job. She had a good reference, and
there were a number of likely offers. She wrote letters,
telephoned, even took long bus journeys in the hope of
getting some work, but luck was against her—she was
too old, too young, lived too far away. At the end of
the following week she was taken on as an interviewer
for a new brand of soap powder, stopping passers-by
and asking for their opinion about rival soap powders.
It was a thankless task: busy housewives didn't want to
stop, young women were flippant, old ladies either chill-
ingly dismissive or garrulous. Besides, it was hard on
the feet and it rained for most of the time, but she was
glad to be earning some money and, more than that, it
was a job of sorts. 'Out of work' sounded so hopeless.

She had been given Southampton Row and
Bloomsbury Way as her stamping ground. The agent who
had employed her had decided that she was pretty and
looked—to use that old-fashioned word—ladylike;
people were more likely to stop for her, especially in that
area.

It was on her last day that Mr van Linssen, driving
himself away from Great Ormond Street hospital, caught
sight of her, standing with her board and pen poised.
He slowed the car, the better to see what she was doing,
and saw her approach a woman with a Harrods bag on
her arm, who halted briefly, waved her away and walked
on. He drew into the side of the road and watched her,
oblivious of the traffic warden making his way towards
him. Eulalia had stopped another woman now, with

more success it seemed, for she was writing something down and the woman was talking.

The warden tapped on the car window and he turned round; at the same time the man saw his 'Doctor on Duty' ticket, nodded and walked away, which left Mr van Linssen free to stare his fill. What was Eulalia doing so far from the flower shop and why was she doing it? He started the car and drove on, already late for the first of his private patients.

It was two days before he could find time to visit the shop, to be greeted by a prim girl with glasses, and as thin as a wafer, a cruel contrast to Eulalia's opulent person.

'Miss Warburton?' he enquired, and Mrs Pearce came from the back of the shop.

'You wanted to speak to Eulalia? I'm afraid I had to dismiss her. One of my best customers complained about her rudeness. She was a very outspoken girl at times, but a good worker.' Her eyes strayed to her new assistant, listlessly bunching stocks.

Mr van Linssen drew a bow at a venture. 'Was the customer by any chance Miss Kendall—my fiancée?'

Mrs Pearce, scenting the likelihood of substantial orders in the future, answered readily. 'Yes—so unfortunate—and I do apologise for Eulalia's sharp tongue. Do you care to order any flowers today?'

He gave her a cold look. 'Thank you, no. I merely wished to speak to Miss Warburton.'

He got back into his car. He had a list that afternoon, and it would be evening before he was free to seek Eulalia out, but he just had time to go and see Ursula before he was due at the hospital.

She was at home, getting ready to go out to lunch with friends.

'Fenno—how lovely—are you free? I'm lunching with the Abbotts and they won't mind if you come with me—we're meeting at Claridge's. You've got your car? Good, I needn't get a taxi.' She stopped and looked at him then. 'What's the matter? You look angry——' she smiled '—but not with me, I hope?'

'Yes, with you, Ursula. Do you know that your complaint about Eulalia at the flower shop resulted in her dismissal? What exactly occurred?'

'Oh, darling, such a fuss about nothing—such an impertinent girl...'

'Why was she impertinent?'

Ursula shrugged. 'Oh, I really can't remember, and she was so clumsy that I dropped the flowers and the vase.' She put a hand on his arm. 'Nothing to worry about, Fenno. Let's go.'

His eyes were hard. 'I'm operating. I'm already in danger of being late. I'll see you some time.'

He left her, and after a minute she shrugged again and told the maid to ring for a taxi. She would have to be extra charming so that he would be his usual patient and tolerant self with her. She was a vain young woman and she had no fear of rivals.

Mr van Linssen, preparing to leave in the late afternoon, found himself back in Theatre once more, dealing with an emergency, and it was late evening by the time he let himself into his house. Dodge, looking more sorrowful than ever, served him his dinner, observed that Miss Kendall had telephoned twice, and expressed the opinion that his master could do with a good night's sleep.

'I shan't be going in to the hospital until the afternoon,' he was told. 'I'll have a quiet morning catching up with the paperwork.'

Dodge shook his head sadly and went away to bring in the coffee-tray. At least his master had shown no desire to phone that Miss Kendall.

Mr van Linssen had his breakfast at the usual time, spent an hour at his desk and then fetched his car and, with a word to Dodge that he would be back for lunch, drove himself away.

I wonder where he's off to? reflected Dodge. Mad as fire, he is. Never a nasty word, but seething all the same.

Mr van Linssen stopped in the Cromwell Road outside Eulalia's flat and went down to its front door, gave the knocker a thump and waited with well-concealed impatience. Trottie opened the door, gave him one look and said, 'Oh, sir...' and then added, 'How nice to see you—you'll come in? I'm doing the housework, if you don't mind the mess.'

He took her hands in his. 'Miss Trott, what has happened? I saw Eulalia near Great Ormond Street hospital, canvassing people. I went to the shop and was informed she had been dismissed. I was told one side of the story, now I want to hear the other.'

Trottie didn't find it strange that he should ask. 'I'll make us a cup of coffee and I'll tell you,' she promised, and presently sat down opposite him. 'Miss Lally's out looking for work. That was only a temporary job, asking people about soap powder—you know—they call it a survey. And I'll tell you why she got sacked, only perhaps I shouldn't, because you may be angry.'

He drank some of his coffee; there was no cake, he noticed. 'No, I promise I won't be that.'

'Well, I don't know what Miss Lally'll say when I tell her—you see, it was things said about you and her, and it was your future intended who said them.'

He smiled at her. 'Miss Trott, if it is what I suspect, then I need to know—is it something Eulalia wouldn't tell me herself even if I asked her?'

'Lord, she'd rather run a mile, sir. That upset she was...' Trottie told him then, and when she'd finished she said, 'So you see how it is, sir, she wasn't going to apologise for something she hadn't said or done.'

'Of course not. I'm sorry this has happened and perhaps it would be better to say nothing to Eulalia. I will forget what you have told me, so that if ever she and I should meet in the future she need never know that I am aware of what was said.' He smiled suddenly. 'And the amusing thing is that she can't stand the sight of me!'

Trottie didn't answer that; sometimes it was best not to interfere with Fate's antics.

'Forgive me for asking, but are the three of you able to manage until she finds another job?'

Trottie was a simple soul and she trusted him. 'Well, Peter's fees are safe—they are in some kind of trust that I don't really understand. We've cut down as much as we can but, you see, we've never been able to save more than a few pounds. It's kind of you to ask, sir, but it's more than my life's worth to accept anything from you— you see that, don't you?'

He nodded. 'Yes, Miss Trott, I do.' A vague, ridiculous plan was taking shape at the back of his head— a pity he had no time to examine it now. He got up, kissed Trottie's elderly soft cheek, left some pocket-money on the table for Peter—and took himself off.

Driving back to his house, he began to laugh. The idea was so preposterous, it might work!

CHAPTER FOUR

MR VAN LINSSEN was unable to pursue his preposterous idea until late that night, when his long day was finished and he was at home sitting at his desk, roughing out a paper on bones which he was to read at a seminar in Holland within the next few weeks. Presently he laid down his pen and sat back and allowed his thoughts to dwell on it. Then he opened his appointment-book and studied it carefully. With a few adjustments and the help of his invaluable secretary, he should be able to give himself a weekend free from patients.

On Friday evening he told Dodge that he would be away for the weekend. 'Ah, yes, sir,' said Dodge, looking more unhappy than ever. 'You will be seeing Miss Kendall?'

'Miss Kendall? No, Dodge, I'm spending it in the Cotswolds.'

He left early on the Saturday morning and drove down the M4 until he turned off for Malmesbury, where he stopped to enquire the way, driving on presently through the quiet countryside through small side-roads until he reached the village he sought—Brokenwell, a fair-sized place with a wide main street, a village green with a cluster of houses, shops and an ancient church. He stopped outside the village pub, the Boy and Horseshoe, and went unhurriedly into the bar where he had coffee, since it was too early for a drink, and enquired if he might stay the night.

There was a room, agreed the landlord, and he was welcome to it.

'Come far, have you, sir?'

'London. I'm looking for someone and I don't know where to start. A family called Warburton lived here, I believe, and I want to get in touch with their solicitor. I don't suppose you could help me?'

'Well, now, that's something I don't know, but if you tried Mrs Tagge at the post office, she'll know, seeing as how she sorts the post and so on.'

Mr van Linssen thanked him, observed that he would be back presently, and crossed the green to the small general stores and post office.

Mrs Tagge was old, rather deaf and short-sighted. That didn't matter, though, as she gave him the information he sought. 'Wanting 'im for a bit of business?' she wanted to know. 'Well-known in these parts, 'e is.'

'So I understand. Thank you, Mrs Tagge.'

He went back to the pub, looked up the solicitor's phone number and dialled it. There was just the chance that there would be someone there on a Saturday morning. There was: the solicitor himself, sounding impatient. 'I'm on the point of going home for the weekend,' he pointed out. 'It would have to be a matter of urgency if you want to see me.'

Mr van Linssen didn't waste his words. 'You were the Warburton family's solicitor, I believe. I know Miss Warburton. She has fallen on hard times and I am anxious to help her, since it is the fault of a close connection of mine that this has happened. I need your help.'

Mr Willett's voice became more friendly. 'Eulalia? Well, yes, I am prepared to see you, Mr—I didn't quite get your name.'

'Van Linssen. When will it be convenient to you? I must be back in London by eight o'clock on Monday morning at the latest. I'm staying at the Boy and Horseshoe.'

'Perhaps you would come to my office this afternoon. Two o'clock. Cirencester—you know the address? Good. I must tell you that this is most unusual, but Eulalia is a dear girl and she hasn't had a very happy life, I imagine, since she left Brokenwell.'

Mr van Linssen agreed, rang off, and took himself off to the pub for bread and cheese and beer, agreed with the landlord that steak and kidney pie with young beans and jacket potatoes would suit him very well that evening, then went to his room—a spotlessly clean apartment, the window of which overlooked the back garden—donned a light jacket and drove himself to Cirencester, a matter of eight miles or so.

Mr Willett was in his office, an elderly man with a serious face. He shook hands, pointed out again that he wasn't in the habit of seeing clients on a Saturday afternoon, but since it was Eulalia... 'You are a friend of hers?'

'Hardly, although we have met. But I am good friends with little Peter.'

'Ah, yes, the little boy who was orphaned. Very sad. She came at once to the rescue, you know. Before we go any further, may I enquire your purpose in helping Eulalia?'

'As I said, it was through a close connection of mine that she lost her job. Peter broke his arm recently and I have been looking after him. It was Miss Trott who told me that they had fallen on bad times.'

'Trottie—of course, she went with Eulalia—a dear soul. You are their doctor?'

'No. I'm in orthopaedics at Maude's. That is how I came to know Peter.'

'Ah, yes, I see. And in what way can I help you?'

'This may sound a little out of the ordinary,' observed Mr van Linssen, 'but if you will hear me out...'

Two hours later he was back at the pub, drinking the strong tea the landlord had offered and eating a lardy cake to go with it. 'Mrs Wedge, the wife that is, is a rare cook. Happen you'll enjoy it, sir.'

Mr van Linssen, contented with his day's work, did.

The next day, Sunday or no Sunday, he was agreeably surprised how willing people were to do business with him when instant payment was offered. No one could have been more helpful than the house agent in Malmesbury, disturbed while browsing over the Sunday papers. He had long ago decided that the cottage this placid gentleman was willing to buy without more ado would never sell—only to a fool who hadn't any idea what it would cost to put it to rights. Although this particular gentleman didn't look like a fool.

Still, business was business. He readily undertook to deal with the purchase as speedily as possible and pocketed Mr van Linssen's cheque before he could change his mind.

Mr van Linssen, aware of the house agent's opinion, smiled to himself and went back to London. He could safely leave the rest to Mr Willett.

Dodge didn't fail to notice his look of satisfaction. 'A pleasant weekend, I trust, sir?' he enquired discreetly.

'Splendid, Dodge, thank you.' He was leafing through the letters and messages on the hall table. There was nothing that required his immediate attention, so he went to his study with the pleasant prospect of a quiet evening and one of Dodge's well-cooked dinners.

The phone rang as he sat down. Ursula, wanting to know where he had been. 'And don't tell me you were at the hospital because they said you weren't.'

'Quite right. I've been out of town on business.'

'What business?'

He was still feeling pleased with himself. 'You don't need to concern yourself with such a dull thing as business, Ursula.'

She gave a tinkling laugh. 'I should hope not. I had a lovely day out in the country—the Thornefolds' place—town's so boring this time of year, darling. Couldn't you take a teeny-weeny holiday? We could have a week or two in the Bahamas. The Thornefolds are going—they've rented a villa on one of those islands. We could be alone.'

Mr van Linssen, without going too deeply into the reason, didn't particularly wish to be alone with his Ursula. 'My dear girl, a holiday, even a couple of days, is quite out of the question. I've an appointment-book bursting at the seams, and besides, I'm due back in Holland within the next week or so. You could come back with me if you like?'

'Don't be silly, Fenno, Holland would be as bad as London—probably worse. All those sausages and cheese...'

He let that pass. She was entitled to her views; perhaps she would alter them when they were married. He frowned at the thought, and said quickly, 'I'll try and get away early tomorrow evening—we might go out to dinner somewhere—in the country, if you like?'

'Oh, all right. Somewhere decent—I don't want to be hemmed in by yokels.' She sounded peevish. 'Call for me about seven-thirty.'

She rang off and he put the phone down, sat down at his desk and opened the first of the folders on it and became immersed at once in its contents, Ursula forgotten, although, strangely enough, the memory of Eulalia standing in a corner of the street with a clipboard, earning a precarious living, persisted in coming between him and the patient's notes before him.

Eulalia had found another job. Putting leaflets about some newfangled washing-machine through letterboxes. Temporary, of course, and she was in a way thankful, for it was boring and tiring and kept her on her feet for the entire day. However she was paid for it—a miserable sum, but better than nothing. It lasted for ten days, and on the day after that, two days before Peter would start his holidays, the postman brought a letter. She didn't open it at once; it was an expensive envelope and it looked official, and she dreaded to open it in case it was some unexpected demand for money. She turned it over in her hand and put it down on the table.

'Go on,' said Trottie, 'open it, Miss Lally.'

The letter inside was on the same expensive paper, and she glanced at the heading and frowned. 'It's from Mr Willett—you remember, Trottie?—our solicitor at Cirencester. Whatever can he be writing about?'

Trottie tutted impatiently. 'Read it and find out,' she suggested.

Eulalia read the letter and then, with a rather pale face, re-read it.

'Trottie,' she said in a strange voice, 'did you know that there was a great-uncle living in Australia? He's died and I'm his only living relation. He's left fifty-six thousand pounds and a cottage in Brokenwell. I don't believe it!'

'If it's from Mr Willett and written in black and white, then you'd best believe it, Miss Lally.'

Eulalia handed over the letter and Trottie got her spectacles and read it in her turn. 'And why not?' she wanted to know. 'There's nothing strange in family going off to the ends of the earth and getting forgotten.' She looked sternly at Eulalia over her glasses. 'And here's me been praying night and day for a bit of help and here it is. You'll go and see Mr Willett, Miss Lally, and take a look at that cottage and see if we can live in it.'

'I'll have to find work, Trottie. I know it seems a lot of money, but the interest won't be enough to live on.' She smiled suddenly. 'Oh, Trottie, if I opened a flower shop...?'

'Just the thing, love. Won't Peter be happy?'

'There's Gormer's close by—a prep school for boys— he could go there!'

'It's meant, Miss Lally. You'd better go tomorrow.'

'Yes, if I catch an early train, I could see Mr Willett first and then take a look at the cottage and come back on the last train.'

'You take care, Miss Lally, it's a wicked world these days.'

Eulalia, her head gloriously filled with rather wild ideas, hardly heard.

Waiting at the school gates for Peter, she wondered what he would say when she told him. Perhaps he might want to stay; he was happy at this school. She need not have doubted his delight when she gave him the news as they walked back to the flat.

'A puppy,' breathed Peter, 'and a cat and a rabbit. Is there a garden, Aunt Lally?'

'I don't know, dear, but I dare say there is. I'm going there tomorrow to have a look. If the cottage is watertight, I dare say we could move into it quite soon.'

He skipped along beside her, full of questions, but presently he said, 'Will you tell Mr van Linssen? He'll want to know; I'm his friend and he'll miss me.'

'He's a busy man, Peter. I know—when we know we're going to move, you can write him a little note and tell him, and thank him for all he's done for you. Will that do?'

He considered. 'Yes, I expect so. I'd like to say goodbye to him.' He brightened. 'He'll want to come and see us before we go.'

'If he has time.'

He wouldn't come, of course, she reflected, he was a busy man; besides, he had his Ursula and his own life and why should he bother? She found herself regretting that.

She caught the earliest possible train to Cirencester the next morning and when she got there went at once to Mr Willett's office. He greeted her warmly, assured her that she was indeed the lawful owner of Ivy Cottage, High Street, Brokenwell, and the sum of fifty-six thousand pounds, and the odd hundred or so, on deposit at the bank. 'And if you should require an advance, Eulalia, I will give you a cheque now. There may be expenses . . .'

'Yes—well, yes, please. I'm out of work and we do need the money. If the cottage is habitable I intend to move in as soon as possible. Peter can start school at Gormer's at the start of the autumn term, if they'll take him, and I'm going to open a flower shop—just a small one. There are several big houses around the village.' She thought briefly of her own old home. 'I might be able to make a living, and there'll be the interest . . .'

'Very prudent,' commented Mr Willett, his hands clasped before him as though in prayer, not inappropriate since he was breathing silent pleas for forgiveness for telling such a pack of lies, even though they were in the best possible interests of the listener.

He gave her coffee, handed her the keys of the cottage, and suggested that when she had been to the bank she might take a taxi to Brokenwell. 'An extravagance,' he said, smiling at her, 'but for once to be condoned.'

Eulalia, with money in her purse, got out of the taxi, paid the driver and stood on the narrow pavement, looking at the property. It was an end cottage, one of a row in the centre of the village, its outside wall overlooking a narrow lane which petered out after a few hundred yards into fields. It looked solid, even if shabby, with a stout door and a window on either side and three smaller windows above. The door opened straight on to the pavement, and after a moment she put the key in the lock and went inside.

There was no hall; she found herself in a small room with faded wallpaper and a Victorian fireplace with an inglenook on either side of it. The door in the opposite wall led straight into the kitchen, its plastered walls discoloured and housing an ancient gas stove and a large white porcelain sink. The back door beside its small window opened on to the garden, and she went outside to have a look. It was in a woeful state, overgrown, with the tin cans and paper bags lying around, but it was quite large, with apple-trees at the end of it and a brick wall surrounding it. She sighed with delight. Peter could have his puppy at last . . .

Inside again, she opened the second door in the living-room to another small room, with the same old-fashioned fireplace and a deep window-seat and a door half-open on to a narrow twisting staircase. She went up slowly and found them solid enough, and at the top there was a tiny landing with three doors. The rooms were small but the views from them were delightful. No bathroom, but then, if she could find someone to put one in for her...

She went out into the main street and walked to the other end and up another small lane, and knocked on the door of a house with a workshop attached. The man who answered it was young, about her age, short and sturdy, with twinkling eyes.

'Lord love us, if it isn't Miss Lally. Here's a sight for sore eyes—come back to live, 'ave yer?'

'Yes. It's Jacob, isn't it?' She held out a hand and had it wrung. 'I wondered if your father could do some work for me.'

'Dad? 'E died two year ago. I'm carrying on the business. What do you want done?'

'I've inherited Ivy Cottage and I want to come and live in it. I haven't much money to spend, but it does need painting and repairing and I want a bathroom built on. Could you do it?'

'Don't see why not, Miss Lally. Tell you what, I'll come with you now and take a look and give you an idea of what it'll cost. It'll be an idea—just a rough one, mind.'

He took some time going over the little house, talking cheerfully all the time. 'The old dodger 'oo 'ad it, he went and died a year ago. Rented it, he did, never bothered much with paint and so on. But it's sound enough, needs a bit of plastering and a lick of paint, and a couple of the windows need to be rehung.'

'And a bathroom?' urged Eulalia.

'Well, now—got to get planning permission for that. Shouldn't be too 'ard, seeing as I'll build it on the back wall the other side of the back door.'

'How long before I could move in?'

'In an 'urry ter come back, are you? Well, we'll all be glad ter see you, Miss Lally. I'm not all that busy—give or take, a couple of weeks ter paint and plaster in and out, take a look at the roof. Don't want no paper on the walls?'

'No, just a nice creamy emulsion—you know—a kind of clotted cream.'

'Just the ticket. The bathroom'll take a bit longer but I could get Jim—the plumber 'oo works for me—ter put a washbasin in one of the bedrooms...'

'All of them, please, and what about hot water?'

'One of them gas boilers. Open fires?'

'Oh, yes. Can you give me some idea of how much it will cost? I know it'll be a rough guess.'

He sat down on the window-seat and produced pencil and paper. The sum he suggested would still leave more than fifty thousand in the bank.

'That's all right. Do you want something on account?'

'It'd be a help.'

She got out her new cheque-book. 'And if I came down in about two weeks, could you advise me about a cooking stove? I've got a washing-machine at the flat in London. It's pretty old but I dare say it'll do for another year or two.' She smiled at him. 'Jacob, it's lovely coming back home. I've still got Miss Trott with me and an orphaned nephew. He's eight, and just longing to get away from London. So are we.' They went out into the street together. 'I'll write to you when we'll be coming to look round, shall I?'

'You do that, Miss Lally. 'Ow you getting back now?'

'I expect there's a bus. I must get back to London this evening.'

'Tell you what, I'll run you back to Cirencester. You wait 'ere, I'll get the van.'

'But it's past your dinnertime.'

'The wife'll keep it 'ot. It's only a few miles anyway.'

She got home late that evening, tired but happy. Jacob had driven her to Cirencester and left her at the railway station and she had had a meal there, decided to take the late afternoon train, and taken herself to look at the shops. Curtains, she had thought happily, and fitted carpets in the bedrooms... By the end of the afternoon she had had a very good idea of what she should buy, and when she had passed the gas showroom windows, she had gone back and entered the shop, chosen a gas cooker and paid for it, feeling reckless.

Recounting her day to the interested Trottie, she observed, 'I do hope I haven't been extravagant, Trottie, but it was reduced because I paid for it at once, and they'll deliver it in a week's time. That'll give Jacob time to get the kitchen painted. Oh, Trottie, it's such a dear little place, I can't believe it's true. We'll be so happy there. It's as though it was meant to happen...'

Mr van Linssen, who had meant it to happen, had a satisfactory talk over the phone with Mr Willett when he got home from the hospital. So far so good...!

The postman came again the next morning, this time with a letter from Eulalia's landlord to inform her that when her lease expired within a few weeks, he regretted having to renew it at a higher rent.

It gave her great pleasure to write and tell him that she wouldn't be renewing the lease.

The next ten days were passed happily enough, plotting and planning about the future: colour schemes were discussed, curtain material decided upon, a furniture remover sought out who would take their household goods as a part-load on his way to Malmesbury and then, assured by Jacob that the cottage was going along nicely, they went, all three of them, to Brokenwell. There was a convenient bus this time, so that they got off in the village just before midday, and as they walked down the street they were stopped by people who remembered them, glad to see them again, so that by the time they reached Ivy Cottage, Peter was dancing with impatience.

It looked quite different now. Jacob had given its walls of Cotswold stone a good clean, painted the door and the windows and replaced the broken gutters. They went inside and found him there, painting the window-seat. He put down his brush as they went in, shook hands with Eulalia and Miss Trott and said, ''Ello, young 'un,' to Peter before taking them on a tour. He had worked miracles, it seemed to Eulalia; the whole place seemed larger now that the walls were painted.

'That's a fine sink,' said Trottie. 'Don't anyone go taking that away.'

'Never worry, Miss Trott, and I'll fix you up a few shelves wherever you want them.'

The bedrooms commanded instant approval. 'May I have a room in the front?' asked Peter. 'I can see right down the street for miles and miles.'

'I don't see why not. Trottie, do you want your room in front or at the back?'

'The back, if it's all the same to everyone. Now I'm up here I'll measure for curtains, and we can get them made before we come.' She took out a tape measure and a notebook and Eulalia took Peter into the garden.

He didn't say anything for a minute, and then looked up at her.

'Yes, dear, just as soon as we're settled in you shall have your puppy.' She was rewarded with a hug.

'And a cat and a rabbit?'

'Yes...'

Jacob asked, 'Likes animals, does 'e? The wife's cat's 'ad kittens. Reckon they'll be ready to leave 'ome by the time you're settled in.' He took some papers out of a pocket. 'I got planning permission—said it was urgent on account of there being no modern sanitary arrangement. Cast your eye over this, Miss Lally, and see if it suits. It'll be easy enough—I can have it done in no time—but it'll cost you a bit more. Got ter have Cotswold stone, you see. The plumber'll be along as soon as I've got it up—starting it tomorrow. The basins in the bedrooms is ready, 'ot water laid on. If you can use the outside convenience for a day or two, you could move in four or five days' time.'

She nodded. 'We'll do that, Jacob. The cottage is finished, isn't it, except for the cooker and the washing-machine? They promised the cooker for Monday—will you be here if they bring it and fit it?'

'Right you are, Miss Lally, I'll be here.'

'You'll need some more money.' She got out her cheque-book once more.

She explored the garden with Peter, discovering hidden rose-bushes, a clump of peonies, lilies, and a neglected strawberry-bed. There were two apple-trees, too, and a plum-tree bowed down with fruit. The brick wall was sound, too, though too high for Peter to see over. It faced south and she thought how it would be a blaze of colour in the spring, with daffodils and grape hyacinths growing at its foot.

Peter flung his arms round her waist. 'Aunt Lally, I'm so happy. Are you happy too?'

'Oh, darling, yes, won't it be fun?'

'Shall I ask Mr van Linssen to come and see us? I expect he'd like to be here and not in London.'

'Well, I'm not sure about that, Peter. You see, he doesn't live our kind of life. He's an important surgeon and has lots of important friends and he's going to be married soon. I doubt if he could spare the time.' Peter's lower lip trembled very slightly and she went on hastily, 'But I'm sure he'd like to have a letter from you.'

'All right. Will you want to read it?'

'No, dear; I'm sure you'll write it very well without any help from me.'

They went back to Cromwell Road that evening, tired and happy, and the next day Eulalia, leaving Peter with Trottie, took herself off to Oxford Street to buy curtain material. There were a lot of windows at the cottage but they were small. She found odd lengths going cheap and bore them back to the flat, where she and Trottie measured and cut, making linings from an old sheet, stitching by hand since they hadn't got a sewing-machine. And by the time they were finished it was time to start packing up.

It was the last day; the van was loaded and the flat empty. Eulalia turned the key in the lock for the last time and without a moment's regret, she told herself, shying away from the unbidden thought that she would have liked to see Mr van Linssen just once more. She still wasn't sure if she liked him, but he had been kind. Besides, she was sorry for Peter, who had looked each day for the Bentley to drive up with him at the wheel, but he hadn't come, nor had he written.

She told herself that a letter from a small boy could easily get overlooked in the mass of his post, but she said nothing to Peter, respecting his unhappy silence.

They would both have felt a lot better if they had known that Mr van Linssen had been to Holland to give urgent advice concerning a rare bone tumour about which he was a well-known authority. Peter's letter was in his pocket, but just for the moment his own affairs had to give way to his work. He operated, stayed long enough to make sure that his patient would make a recovery, and returned to England four days after Eulalia had moved to Brokenwell.

Any unhappy feelings they had were for the time swallowed up in the excitement of the move. Jacob had worked wonders with the cottage. The gas cooker had been installed, there were shelves in the kitchen just where Trottie wanted them, and washbasins in the bedrooms, and the chimney-sweep had been. It was late evening before they had got the beds up and made, the elderly, still handsome, Turkey carpet from their old home laid in the sitting-room and the more immediate necessities of life unpacked. They sat around the kitchen table eating beans on toast and drinking tea, before seeing a sleepy Peter into his bed.

'When can I have a bath?' he wanted to know.

'Tomorrow. We'll go over to the Boy and Horseshoe. Jacob says the landlord—Mr Wedge—will let us have baths until the bathroom is ready.'

Later Eulalia eagerly inspected the almost completed extension to the back of the cottage. It was small, just room for its basic equipment, but never mind its austerity, she thought, it was all they needed to make the cottage perfect.

They hung curtains the next morning, rearranged what furniture they had, and cleaned and polished until Trottie pronounced herself satisfied that there wasn't a speck of dust or dirt to be found, and, when Peter had arranged his toys in the cupboard in his bedroom, they had coffee then went into the back garden and spent an hour picking up the rubbish.

'I'll have to buy some garden tools,' said Eulalia, handing Jacob and his mate their elevenses.

'There's a car-boot sale on Saturday,' Jacob told her. 'You might pick up a spade and suchlike. Old Bob—remember him? He's still doing an odd job on and off, as you might say. He'd come and clear the garden for a fiver. Scythe down the grass and clear the worst of the weeds.'

'Would he? Is he still living in Water Lane? I'll go and see him.'

They went over to the Boy and Horseshoe presently and had their baths and a hot meal and, leaving Trottie to go back to the cottage, Eulalia and Peter went to call on old Bob—not all that old and still very fit.

'I heard you was back, Miss Lally, love. Plenty of us old uns remember you and your granny up at the 'ouse. In Ivy Cottage, are you? Nice little place and very sound. I'll be along one day and take a hand to that garden. Nice enough it was once—got a bit neglected.'

'Yes, I know, but if you'd give it a start I intend to get it going again. There's any amount of stuff swallowed up with weeds.'

He nodded. 'Couple of good apple-trees...'

'And a plum and a row of soft-fruit bushes...'

They nodded in agreed enthusiasm.

In two days they were more or less straight, with curtains at the windows, chairs and tables finally in the right

places, and cupboards and drawers filled from the
packing-cases; moreover, the bathroom was finished.
Eulalia surveyed it with a pride tinged with regret that
having the walls tiled and the floor laid was for the
moment beyond the budget she had allowed herself. But
she promised herself she would go to Cirencester to buy
bright-coloured towels and a bathmat to give it an air
of warmth.

She paid Jacob and the plumber and sat down to count
her money. There was still some over without touching
the fifty thousand in the bank. In a week or two, once
they were settled in and she had arranged Peter's school,
she would see if Jacob could turn the decrepit old shed
halfway down the garden into something watertight
where she could start her flower shop. Life was full of
possibilities—Trottie was happy renewing old acquaintances in the village, and Peter was in the seventh heaven,
and as for herself—she was happy too. She found herself
wishing she could tell Mr van Linssen just how happy
she was.

A wish which was to be granted.

Mr van Linssen, back home again, immersed himself
immediately in his work, spending long hours in the operating theatre, taking over Outpatients from his
registrar, catching up with his private patients at his consulting-rooms. It was only when he had dealt satisfac-
torily with all these things that he permitted himself to
think about Eulalia. She would have moved by now, of
course. He phoned Mr Willett and was told that, yes,
Eulalia had taken up residence at Ivy Cottage. She would
be going to see Mr Willett some day next week. 'She has,
I hear, made the place very attractive, knows exactly what

she wants and goes after it. Very like her grandmother,' added Mr Willett drily.

Ursula, peevish at Mr van Linssen's determination to keep his handsome nose to the grindstone, had taken herself off with friends to the south of France, so he felt free to plan a day's outing to Brokenwell. He had to explain to Peter why he hadn't answered his letter, besides that he had a present for him.

It was a fine morning when he set out, and the traffic was heavy since it was a Saturday; all the same, he drew up at Ivy Cottage soon after ten o'clock. Peter, hanging out of his bedroom window, saw him at once and raced downstairs. 'Aunt Lally, he's here, I knew he'd come...' He opened the cottage door and flung himself at Mr van Linssen, which gave Eulalia time to peer into the little looking-glass in the kitchen and deplore her shining nose and untidy head of curls, but there was no time to do more than switch off the iron and go to meet him.

Her, 'Good-morning, Mr van Linssen,' was pleasantly friendly and was answered by his cheerful,

'Hello, Eulalia,' and a quick kiss on her cheek.

She ignored that, aware that her heart was thumping far too loudly. 'How did you know where we were?'

'Your landlord gave me the forwarding address.' He was a truthful man, but the lie slipped off his tongue without trouble; if he told the truth he would involve Mr Willett, who would never forgive him.

'Well, now you're here,' said Eulalia in a cool voice, 'will you have a cup of coffee? Trottie's shopping—she will be back presently and will be glad to see you.' She went a little pink at his amused look, and added clumsily, 'Well, we are all glad to see you. Do come in.'

'Thank you, but first I have something for Peter.' He went back to the car, and when he turned round there was a small puppy under his arm.

CHAPTER FIVE

'I HAD your letter, Peter and thank you for it. I had to go to Holland for a while and had no chance to answer it, and when I got back I had rather a lot of work to do. I hope this little fellow will recompense you for your disappointment.'

'A puppy,' shouted Peter. 'For me? For my very own? I can keep him?'

Mr van Linssen put the little creature into Peter's arms. 'If Eulalia will allow you to keep him, he's yours.'

The puppy peered from under his arm, his round eyes wary. He was of no known breed, with large ears and a rough black coat with a white shirt-front. Eulalia reflected that Mr van Linssen hadn't put a foot wrong; someone less understanding might have turned up with a pedigree pup, but he had known just the kind of dog a small boy would want. She said quietly, 'Of course Peter may have him, it's one of his dreams come true. He's a darling little dog.'

She watched the small creature in Peter's arms, wriggling a little and then licking the small hand which held him. 'He likes me,' said Peter in a satisfied voice. 'Thank you very much, Mr van Linssen, he's just exactly what I would have chosen. Has he got a name?'

'Not yet, that's for you to decide, isn't it? I've brought his basket with me, and there's a little book telling you how to feed him and take care of him...'

He was still standing at the door, and Eulalia said quickly, 'Do please come in.'

'Thank you, and coffee would be delightful. I'll get the basket first, shall I?'

He came back from the car with it, carrying a box too. 'I wasn't sure whether you could get the right food, so I brought some with me.'

He followed her into the cottage with Peter keeping close, cuddling the puppy.

Trottie, returning from her shopping trip, came up behind them.

'Well, this *is* a lovely surprise. Sit yourself down, love—coffee's soon ready, and one of my cakes. Come far, have you?'

He bent to kiss her cheek. 'What a lovely warm welcome,' he observed, and Eulalia blushed. She had been lacking in manners; he must think her rude.

She said on an impulse, 'I'm sorry I wasn't more welcoming, Mr van Linssen, I—I was surprised.'

Trottie had gone to fetch the coffee and Peter had gone into the garden with the puppy. Mr van Linssen loomed over her. 'Oh, good—I thought for a moment that your strong feelings had got the better of you and you were going to show me the door.'

'That's absurd, besides, you brought the puppy and made Peter so happy.'

He smiled a little. 'And you, Eulalia, are you happy?' He looked around the comfortable little room. 'This is a charming little cottage, a far cry from Cromwell Road. Did you win the pools? The letter I had from Peter left me rather in the dark.'

She was very conscious of his nearness. 'It seems that I had a great-uncle in Australia, who left me the cottage and quite a lot of money—there isn't anyone else in the family, you see. I'd never heard of him, but he has my eternal thanks.' She drew rather a defiant breath. 'I'm going to open a shop—a flower shop.'

'What a splendid idea. Here in the village?'

She nodded. 'Not just yet, of course, but I'll have to make a living of some sort later on. There are any number of large houses scattered around, if I could get them interested, and there'll be weddings and funerals.'

He didn't say what he thought about her plans but bent and kissed her cheek very gently. 'I'm so glad you have had good luck for a change.' He moved away from her and added lightly, 'You don't mind me calling? I had to put matters right with Peter, but I promise you I won't bother you again.'

Before she could answer that, Trottie came in with the coffee. 'You'll stop for lunch,' she told him, and didn't look at Eulalia. 'Cold chicken and a salad and jacket potatoes, and an apple pie for afters.'

'Delicious. Thank you, Miss Trott, I should like that very much. And how do you like this village?'

'Bless you, love, I was born here, know every stick and stone in it, not to mention them as lives here.'

'Indeed?' He turned an enquiring face to Eulalia. 'So that is why you decided to come and live here. I suppose you could have sold the cottage and found something else.'

She handed him a slice of cake on a plate. 'As a matter of fact, I lived here too,' she told him. Her manner dared him to ask more questions.

He looked politely surprised. 'Well, well, that must be delightful for you. The village is well away from the main roads, isn't it?'

They discussed the surrounding countryside for a while until he said, 'May I find Peter and talk to him about the puppy? He's a bright little boy, but I'd better explain feeding times and so on.'

He took himself off to where Peter sat with his new companion, eating cake, sharing the slice between them. The garden was still unkempt and overgrown, but Peter had found an old wooden bench and Mr van Linssen sat down beside him. The bench groaned under his weight but didn't collapse, and the pair of them stayed there until Trottie called them in for their lunch.

'Wash your hands,' she warned them. 'There's our nice bathroom so you've no excuse.'

Mr van Linssen, meekly doing as he was told, looked around him. It was a very basic new bathroom, he considered, but Eulalia seemed to be managing very well. The cottage was repaired and painted but she hadn't wasted money on unnecessary furbishing. He wasn't sure about her plans for a flower shop, but it would be best not to mention it at the moment—he was, after all, supposed to have only a passing interest, and when he had said that he wouldn't come to see her again she hadn't replied...

He left shortly after their meal, saying all the right things to Trottie and kissing her elderly cheek, shaking hands with Peter and bidding Eulalia a coolly friendly goodbye which left her in no doubt about not seeing him again. Which was exactly what he had intended...

Watching the Bentley's elegant rear disappearing down the street, she reflected that he couldn't have made himself more plain; this had been by way of a farewell visit for Peter's sake. Certainly he had spent a good deal of time with the little boy, sitting out there in the garden. She wondered what they had talked about.

She went back into the cottage and helped with the washing-up, and then wandered into the garden where Peter was playing with the puppy.

'I must think of a name,' said Peter, 'and when I have I shall write and tell Mr van Linssen about it.'

'Well, dear...' began Eulalia, not quite sure how to go on.

'Don't you like him?'

'Yes, yes, of course I do, but I think he brought you the puppy as a kind of goodbye present, don't you?'

He shook his head. 'He's my friend.'

'That's nice—to have a friend, I mean. You must think of a really good name. I'll think, too, while I do a bit of gardening.'

She wasn't thinking about names as she toiled away at clearing the fruit-bushes, though, she was remembering Mr van Linssen's casual goodbye, and why she should mind that he had been so casual she didn't know. She attacked a gooseberry-bush quite fiercely, and told herself not to waste time thinking about someone who didn't matter at all when there were so many other important matters to decide upon.

They all went to church on Sunday morning, leaving the puppy happily asleep in his basket in the kitchen, and because there was a new rector since Eulalia had lived there with her grandmother, and several people in the congregation wanted to speak to her, their progress was slow as they left after the service. Peter said nothing, but the hand she was holding squeezed hers once or twice, just to remind her that he wanted to get back to his new companion, so she made the excuse that she had to get back to cook the Sunday dinner and left Trottie happily renewing old acquaintances.

'I've thought of a name,' said Peter as they reached the cottage. 'Charlie.'

'Just right,' declared Eulalia. 'Put on your sandals, dear, and take him into the garden and tell him.'

So Charlie became one of the family, and she thought of Mr van Linssen every time she looked at him.

It was during the following week that Jacob arrived with a ginger kitten tucked inside his jersey. 'A little lady,' he pointed out. 'As sweet a nature as you'd wish for. I heard as how you'd got a pup, so they'll be friends, like.'

Peter was over the moon. 'Aunt Lally,' he said excitedly, 'now we've got all we wanted, haven't we? Well, almost—there's still the rabbit and, of course, I would like you to have a big Bentley motor car like Mr van Linssen.'

'I'll settle for the rabbit,' declared Eulalia, not altogether truthfully.

After suitable correspondence, she took him to the new school, enrolled him for the autumn term and set about getting his uniform. That meant two or three trips to Cirencester with a Peter impatient to get back to his pets. He had named the kitten Blossom, and there was no denying the fact that he was now a very happy and contented small boy.

'It is such a pity that I shall never be able to thank that great-uncle,' she told Trottie one day. 'Just think, Trottie, we might still have been in Cromwell Road trying to find somewhere to live and me hunting for work. Which reminds me, once we've got Peter settled at school I must start thinking about the shop. You still think it's a good idea?'

Trottie nodded. 'It's worth a try. Start in a small way and see how it goes. You'll have to give it a year, and if it's paying its way by then you can open up a bit.'

Eulalia gave her a hug. 'Trottie, what would we do without you?' She stretched her arms open wide. 'Oh, isn't life just wonderful?'

'Never better, Miss Lally. All we want now is for some nice young man to come along and sweep you off your feet.'

'He'd need plenty of strength! I'm what is politely known as generously built, Trottie, and he'd have to be someone special, for he'd have to take Peter and you as well as me, not to mention Charlie and Blossom.' She sighed. 'He'd be hard to find.'

'That's as may be, but you ought to have a nice young man to take you out a bit, Miss Lally.'

'I'm very happy,' said Eulalia, and almost believed it. She had no right to be otherwise; everything she had wished for had come true, so why should she hanker after seeing Mr van Linssen again? Such a hopeless wish it was best forgotten at once.

She went into the garden and went on with clearing the fruit-bushes. With luck, they would have soft fruit enough next year, and very soon they could pick the apples. The plums were ripe, too; they were eating them every day and Trottie was in her element turning them into jam.

'I have no reason to feel the least bit unhappy,' said Eulalia to Charlie, who was helping her with the digging after his own fashion.

Most of the younger men and women Eulalia had known when she had lived with her grandmother were either married or had left home, but there were still one or two left. Once Peter was going to school she would accept their invitations for coffee or a game of tennis or supper. It would be very pleasant to renew old friendships, she reflected, and since Peter would have his lunch at school he would be away all day during the week. The rector's small son was already at the school, and the rector had suggested that he could give Peter a lift there and back when he took his own son, an offer which she had thankfully accepted.

By the time Peter's school started the autumn term, they had settled into a pleasant routine. Trottie, back in her own village, was shedding the years, going off to the village shops, cooking and bottling and making jam from the blackberries Eulalia and Peter had picked to go with the apples. As for Peter, he had filled out nicely, made friends in the village, and spent happy hours training Charlie and playing with Blossom. He was looking forward to school, too, his one regret that he couldn't take his pets with him.

'Well, dear,' said Eulalia cheerfully, 'you will be here to give them their breakfasts in the morning and take Charlie into the garden, and back here to give them their supper, and we might take Charlie for a walk before your supper.'

Peter, a reasonable child, agreed to this, only adding, 'It's a pity that Mr van Linssen can't see Charlie. You don't suppose he'll come to see us?'

'No, love, I don't expect that he will. He'll be getting married soon and he won't have any time.'

'He could write a little letter...'

'Important people like him have secretaries to write their letters.'

She went with the rector on Peter's first day at school, careful to keep in the background—small boys, she knew, were touchy about grown-ups tagging along. From a distance, she saw him and the rector's son go through the imposing front door of the school. 'I do hope he'll be happy,' she told her companion.

'No doubt of it! He's a happy child and well-liked. I'll bring him home with my son Jack this afternoon, and you'll find he's settled in without any trouble. You'll have more time to yourself now, won't you? You must come over to the Rectory for a game of tennis one afternoon. Do you remember the Woollands? Victor and Joyce have been in America but they're due back any day now—nice to meet old friends again...'

'Yes, I did know them—but not very well.' She hadn't liked Joyce much, a gushing girl who spread spiteful gossip, and as for Victor, unless he had improved out of all knowledge, she had no particular wish to see him again. He had had damp hands and an overpowering conceit. She couldn't refuse the rector's invitation, however. He had been very kind, helping her to slip into village life again, and perhaps Victor had improved since they had last seen each other...

She met him in the village street a few days later, and at first glance he didn't appear to have altered at all, and his hand when he grasped hers was still damp. 'Lally, we were told you were back—come into a fortune, I hear. Some people have all the luck!' He laughed heartily and she smiled a polite smile and hastened to disillusion him.

'Whatever you heard is nonsense, Victor. I've inherited Ivy Cottage and some money from a relative.'

He sniggered. 'Didn't suppose you'd admit it. Never very forthcoming, were you? Still got that boy with you?'

'Peter? Yes, and Miss Trott.'

'Nosy old bird...'

She fired up. 'How dare you talk like that of Miss Trott? I must be on my way. Give my love to Joyce...'

He put a hand on her arm. 'Got off on the wrong foot. Sorry, old girl. Just my joking. No offence. Joyce'll

want to see you—may we come and see you one day?
Renew old friendships, eh?'

She said levelly, 'We never were friends, Victor, but
do bring Joyce if she would like to come.'

She told Trottie when she got back to the cottage. 'I
couldn't refuse him, could I?' she asked. 'We used to
play tennis together, but then there were the Cartwrights
and the Kingsleys, so I never had much to do with Victor
or Joyce. He behaved as though we'd been the best of
friends instead of casual acquaintances.'

'Who is spreading tales about your fortune, I'd like
to know?'

'I don't suppose anyone is. I think he was trying to
find out if I'd come into a lot of money.'

Trottie snorted. 'Like his cheek, I never did like those
two, Miss Lally. I remember them when they were quite
small—a pair of mischief-makers, they were.'

'Well, we don't have to bother about them, Trottie. I
expect they've got jobs and won't be around much.'

Wishful thinking. Joyce intended to stay at home for
a while, declaring that her visit to the United States had
unsettled her, and Victor, who had some mysterious job
in Bristol, told anyone who asked him that he had been
given leave in order to recover from some complaint
which he didn't specify.

They came to see Eulalia one morning, and she gave
them coffee and listened politely to their colourful accounts of their stay in America, regretted when asked
that she was far too busy to return their visit at the
moment, and hoped that she had seen the last of them.
But they came again, and then Victor took to coming
on his own and, never mind if she was gardening or busy
about the cottage, he stood around, getting in her way

until she begged him as nicely as possible not to call so often.

He had laughed that off with a speaking look. 'Oh, look, now Eulalia, we're old friends. I'm keen to resume our friendship and go a bit further.'

Her grey eyes flashed. 'That's a very silly remark; we never were friends, or have you forgotten? The odd game of tennis, seeing each other in other people's houses from time to time—so there's nothing to resume and certainly no reason for you to "go a bit further", whatever you may mean by that.'

'I'm thinking of settling down, Lally, and I've decided that I might marry you.'

'Don't call me Lally, and I don't care in the least what you have decided. I wouldn't marry you if you were the last man left on earth.'

He took it as a joke. 'Oh, come on, old girl. I'm quite a catch, you know—a fairly decent job, and there'll be some money when Mother and Father die, and until then we'll have your little nest-egg to fall back on.'

She looked at him with horror. 'What a perfectly dreadful thing to say. What gave you the idea that you could live off what you call my "little nest-egg"? Of all the colossal cheek. Go away, Victor, and stop bothering me. I don't like you and I'll be obliged if you don't come here again.'

He looked put out, but only for a moment. 'Taken you by surprise, haven't I? Think it over, Lally. Your future isn't exactly anything to get excited about, is it?'

'Get out,' said Eulalia. 'You're so conceited you can't see when you're not wanted or liked. Don't come back, either.' As he turned to go she added, 'And don't dare to call me Lally—that's only for my nearest and dearest.'

After he'd gone she stayed in the garden for a while; it would never do to upset Trottie. She dismissed his visit lightly when that lady asked what he had wanted and it wasn't until Peter was in bed that evening that Trottie said severely, 'I would like to know now, Miss Lally, what's upset you. It's that Victor, isn't it?'

So Eulalia told her, unaware that Peter was sitting at the top of the staircase listening to every word.

'He's pestering me, Trottie,' said Eulalia. 'He's got the idea that I've plenty of money and he thinks he can marry me and live on it—probably he'll want to live in this cottage too. I don't know what to do.'

Peter did, however. He crept back to bed and lay awake, his arm around Charlie. Here was a reason to write to Mr van Linssen, who had written his name and address and telephone number on a little card and given it to him when they had been in the garden together. It was a secret, he had said, just between the two of them, and if he was needed Peter was to write to him or telephone and he would come. 'You see,' Mr van Linssen had explained, 'Eulalia and Trottie haven't a man to look after them—you are a splendid help to them, but sometimes a man is needed.'

They had shaken hands on it.

Telephoning would be difficult but he could write a letter. He had enough money for a stamp, and when there was no one to see he took paper and an envelope from the kitchen drawer. He wrote it sitting up in bed the next night, addressed it carefully, stamped it and, when he went to the village shop with Lally after school, he posted it while she was buying the bacon Trottie wanted.

Mr van Linssen, coming down to an early breakfast, found it beside his plate with the rest of his post and opened it first. He read the childish writing, frowning, and then giving a snort of laughter at Peter's urgent PS begging him to come quickly and marry his aunt Lally before Victor could!

He put the letter aside then and read the rest of his mail, applied himself to his breakfast and went to his study where he rang his secretary. That highly efficient lady listened to him without comment and then said, 'Well, Mr van Linssen, I'll do my best. You're due at the hospital in half an hour and I presume you will be there for most of the day. I'll contact your private patients with appointments for tomorrow morning and arrange for them to come on the following day or this evening. You have an outpatients clinic tomorrow afternoon at five o'clock.'

He thought for a moment. 'Do that, will you? I should be back some time during the late afternoon. I'll phone you then. Let me know later on how many patients will be coming this evening, will you?'

Dodge bowed a sorrowful head when he was told that his master would require breakfast at seven o'clock on the following morning. 'I need to go to the country, Dodge, but I should be back around four o'clock.'

'As you say, sir. May I remind you that you are taking Miss Kendall to lunch tomorrow?'

Mr van Linssen swore powerfully in his own language. 'Ring her, will you, Dodge? Tell her that I've been called away on urgent business.'

Dodge's voice was as mournful as it always was, but he hid a pleased smile. Miss Kendall didn't like him; indeed, he thought it likely that when she married Mr van Linssen she would see that he was dismissed. An observant man, he thought he had detected a certain reluctance on the part of Mr van Linssen to join in any of the social activities which his fiancée found so vital to her enjoyment of life. She would certainly be extremely put out, he reflected with relish, closing the door after his master.

Mr van Linssen worked his way through the day, operating all the morning, doing a ward round in the afternoon and then going straight to his consulting-rooms to see his private patients. It was almost eight o'clock by the time he put the key in his front door, to be met by Dodge with the observation that dinner would be on the table in twenty minutes or so, and would he like a drink at once?

'Give me ten minutes. I'll have a shower and change. No messages?'

'No, sir. I telephoned Miss Kendall and apprised her of the situation.'

'And?'

'She was a little put out, if I may say so, but will telephone you tomorrow evening.'

Mr van Linssen grunted a reply and took himself off upstairs, to come down presently, have a drink and eat his dinner, and now that he was free from his work he applied himself to the problem of Eulalia. She was becoming a liability, he told himself, and was quite old enough to take care of herself, but Peter's letter couldn't be ignored. It was best that he went to Brokenwell and saw what was happening for himself. Victor might be quite a decent chap, to whom Peter had taken a dislike, probably at the idea of his aunt getting married.

The September morning held a touch of chilliness as he got into his car and drove away. It was eight o'clock and the morning traffic was building up, but once he was free of the suburbs he sent the Bentley surging ahead. It was good to be free of London, even if only for a few hours, and it would be good to see Eulalia again, tiresome girl though she was.

He slowed the car through the village street very soon after ten o'clock and stopped before Ivy Cottage. The door was open and Trottie was polishing the brass knocker. Her nice elderly face creased into a wide smile as he got out. 'Well, I never did. Now, isn't this nice, and just in time for a cup of coffee. Peter's at school but Miss Lally's in the garden.' The smile went for a moment. 'That Victor's with her again. It don't matter what she says, he pesters her something shocking. Keep the front door locked and he climbs the fence into the back garden, if you please.'

Mr van Linssen bent to kiss her cheek. 'Ah, Victor— I hoped that I would meet him.'

'Is that why you're here? How did you know?'

'I think that had better be a secret, Miss Trott. Do you suppose that I might go into the garden?'

'You do that, my love. I don't doubt Miss Lally will be glad to see you.'

'The lesser of two evils?' suggested Mr van Linssen with a smile, and opened the back door.

Lally was at the bottom of the garden, picking the last of the apples, and Victor was leaning against a tree, facing the cottage, so that he saw Mr van Linssen first. Eulalia, who had been telling him in a forthright manner just what she thought of him, saw the look of surprise on his face and turned round to look herself. Mr van Linssen, treading lightly despite his size, was within a foot of her.

Before he could speak he had reached her, put a great arm round her shoulders and said breezily, 'Lally, my dear, I intended to phone you when I got back, but I thought I would surprise you.' He dropped a kiss on her cheek for good measure. 'Is this by any chance Victor, who has been so tiresome in his attentions?' He shook his head slowly. 'Really, young man, you must know by now that they are unwelcome. I suggest, in the friendliest manner, mind you, that you leave Eulalia alone— you mustn't poach on another man's preserves, you know.'

He smiled in a kindly way, aware of Eulalia bursting with rage at being called a preserve. 'I take it you understand me?' He was still smiling but his eyes were like cold steel, and Victor muttered that he was just going anyway.

'Good, good, and stay away, won't you?' suggested Mr van Linssen in the silkiest of voices. 'I trust that I have made myself plain?'

Victor mumbled again and hurried away, to be met at the kitchen door and ushered out of the cottage without waste of time by Trottie, who had been watching from the kitchen window. It was a pity that she had been unable to hear what had been said, but no doubt Miss Lally would tell her later. She took a newly baked cake out of the pantry and set it on the kitchen table with the coffee-cups, humming cheerfully.

Eulalia and Mr van Linssen watched Victor hurry away before she turned to face him. He spoke first. 'I must apologise for referring to you as my preserve—it seemed the best way of making that oaf understand.'

Having cut the ground neatly from under her feet, he waited quietly for her to speak. 'Yes, well, it did annoy me. It made me sound like a—a...'

'Preserve? Make no mistake, Eulalia, I could never think of you in that light. What a tiresome fellow he is.'

'Tiresome? Tiresome?' She was still angry and humiliated at having been found and taken by surprise.

'He's been the bane of my life.' She added defiantly, 'I've never encouraged him...'

'Well, no, I don't doubt that.' His tone was dry and she looked at him.

'Why are you here?'

'The warmth of your welcome flatters me, Eulalia!'

She went pink. 'I do beg your pardon, that was dreadfully rude. I'm a bit upset.' She gave a great sniff and looked away. 'Do you suppose he'll stay away from me now?'

'Yes. I think that I have given him to understand that I have—er—a prior claim.'

The pink which was ebbing away came flooding back. 'That's nonsense.'

'Of course it is. We must not forget that I am to be married at some future date, but this Victor doesn't need to know that, does he?'

'Well, it was very kind of you to—to pretend...' She paused and went on in a polite voice. 'I am most grateful to you, Mr van Linssen. Perhaps you would like a cup of coffee?'

'Thank you.' They started walking towards the kitchen door. 'Tell me, how is Peter enjoying his school?'

'He loves it, and he loves Charlie—the puppy. Trottie's got him in the sitting-room because he tried to bite Victor the other day.'

'Ah! I thought he was an intelligent dog when I got him!'

It seemed important to keep some sort of a conversation going. 'Do you have a dog?'

'Yes, in Holland. I live there for the greater part of the year.'

They had paused at the kitchen door. 'Do you?' asked Eulalia blankly. 'I thought you lived in London.'

He answered her gravely. 'When I am over here working, yes, I do.'

For some reason she felt snubbed, but some contrary imp moved her to ask, 'So Miss Kendall will live in Holland. Will she like that?'

He only smiled at her, so that she felt even more snubbed than before. Well, it had been silly of her to ask questions. She lifted her chin and invited him into the cottage.

The coffee was already on the table, and so was one of Trottie's cakes, already cut into generous slices. She poured his coffee, offered him cake and asked artlessly, 'Having a bit of a holiday, Mr van Linssen?'

'No, no, just a morning off. London is a delightful city, but now and again a breath of country air is pleasant.' He turned to Eulalia. 'Do you suppose that if I were to drive over to Peter's school I might be allowed to see him for a few minutes?'

'I don't know. They're a bit strict about strangers—not that you're a stranger, but they wouldn't know that.'

'In that case, perhaps you would phone them from the car and vouch for me? I can't come all this way without seeing him.'

They went out to the car presently and she phoned the headmaster and explained. 'And please don't tell Peter. Mr van Linssen would like to surprise him.'

So he went away shortly after that, saying that he'd call in to say goodbye on his way back, refusing Trottie's offer of steak and kidney pudding and one of her apple pies with real regret.

He was back within the hour, to stay only long enough to thank Trottie for the coffee and cake and express his hope to Eulalia that she would no longer be bothered by Victor's unwelcome attentions.

She brushed that aside. 'You saw Peter? He was surprised?'

He looked down at her pretty face, smiling a little. 'He seemed glad to see me. He looks very well. Country air suits him. It suits you too, Eulalia.'

He stood, still looking at her, and she thought with a pleasant little thrill that he was going to kiss her. He didn't, however, but got into the Bentley and drove away.

CHAPTER SIX

'WERE you surprised to see Mr van Linssen?' Eulalia asked Peter when he got home from school that afternoon.

'Yes, I was, but I did know he'd come and see me again, Aunt Lally.' He gave her a guileless look.

Mr van Linssen had told him that he had done quite the right thing in writing to him: 'For your aunt Lally mustn't be bothered by uncouth fellows like this Victor. Remember, Peter, that I will always come if you or she needs me.' He had smiled at the small trusting face lifted to his. 'You're happy here? I saw Charlie—he looks splendid, and Blossom is just the right companion for him.' He had told Mr van Linssen that he was very happy, adding that sometimes his aunt Lally looked sad.

'I suppose you can't do anything about that?' he had asked.

Mr van Linssen had looked grave. 'I think that perhaps in time I might be able to do just that,' he had said. He had gone away then, after slipping a pound into Peter's hand.

Of course, he wasn't going to tell Aunt Lally about their conversation, not that part of it, at any rate.

As for Trottie, she kept her own counsel. Gentlemen, especially those who had important jobs and were engaged to be married, didn't drive miles just to drink her coffee and eat her cake and arrive just when they were most needed... Someone had told him about Victor. She glanced at Peter, sitting at the table, doing sums. When presently Eulalia said suddenly, 'How did Mr van Linssen know about Victor?' she sounded suspicious. Trottie said comfortably, 'The world's a small place, love. I dare say he met up with someone from round about here who mentioned it—you know what people are—and the rector was in London a week or so ago. Probably they go to the same club.'

A most unlikely thing, but since Eulalia knew as little about London clubs as Trottie did she agreed readily enough.

As for Mr van Linssen, he drove himself back to London, had the tea the faithful Dodge had ready for him, changed from country tweeds into sober grey suiting and equally sober silk tie, and took himself off to his clinic in Outpatients. He was invariably pleasant and very civil to those who worked with and for him, but today there was a warmth in his manner which surprised them. Outpatients Sister, a comfortable fortyish woman and married, remarked on it to her staff nurse.

'Perhaps he's in love.'

'Out of the question. He's engaged to that hoity-toity young woman who came last Christmas to see the decorations. A toffee-nosed creature she was, too.'

'He could still have fallen in love,' said the staff nurse shrewdly.

'And serve her right,' observed Sister.

Mr van Linssen was home again by seven o'clock, in time to change yet again, this time into a black tie, since he was invited with Ursula to a dinner party with some friends of hers. He had no wish to go, but he had seen very little of her lately and he must make amends.

She was looking particularly charming that evening in a dress of bright blue, the colour of her eyes, cut very low, which was a mistake, for her figure was what she described as boyish and the dress did nothing for her flat chest. Whatever Mr van Linssen's thoughts were about it he didn't give voice to them, but expressed a liking for the colour of the dress and suggested that they should be on their way.

'I've not had you to myself for days,' pouted Ursula, offering a cheek for his kiss, 'and do be careful of my hair, Fenno...'

He was acquainted with almost everyone there. His host and hostess were Americans who lived for a good part of the year in London in a large house in Hampstead, and their guests were as cosmopolitan as they were. Mr van Linssen's perfect manners concealed his boredom as he greeted everyone in turn, while Ursula flitted from one group to the next, trilling her light laugh, making amusing conversation, in her element. Watching her flirting with a youngish American he didn't know, he tried to imagine her as his wife and found it impossible.

Driving her back to her home later, he answered her remarks about their evening in an absent-minded manner so that she said crossly, 'Well you make it sound as though the whole evening was a bore. You really are getting a bore yourself, Fenno. Once we're married, I intend to entertain a lot—I've heaps of friends. Think how influential they will be—you'll get well known, you might even get a knighthood.'

He forbore to tell her that he was already well known in the medical world—a world which mattered to him; besides, how could he, a Dutchman be offered a knighthood? If his services to surgery ever merited it, then his own queen would reward him for them. He was suddenly tired, too tired to argue with Ursula. He saw her into her home, wished her goodnight, refusing an offer to go in for a cup of coffee, and drove himself to his own home, thankful that he had several appointments in Holland and would be leaving on the following day for a week or more.

He phoned Ursula when he got in and listened patiently while she grumbled at him for not letting her know sooner. 'That nice man I was talking to—he's from Chicago—invited us both to have lunch with him on Sunday. He's rented an apartment in Richmond while he's staying here—I said we would go, and now you've spoilt it all.'

'I am sorry I forgot to tell you. There's no reason why you shouldn't go without me, is there? Make my apologies. I cannot change any of the appointments I've made in Holland.'

'Oh, well, I'll go on my own—there'll be several of us there.' She added peevishly, 'You won't be able to carry on like this when we're married, you know.'

She rang off and he went along to his study to catch up on his paperwork. Then, after a busy day on the morrow, he caught an evening flight to Schiphol, where he was met by a grey-haired man who shook his hand and led him outside to where a dark blue Jaguar was parked.

Mr van Linssen, reverting to his mother tongue, remarked that it was nice to be back home. 'Everyone well, Pete?' he wanted to know as he took the wheel.

'*Mevrouw* arrived this afternoon. She hopes to see something of you while you are here, *mijnheer*, and that you will have time to see the rest of the family.'

'I shall be busy, Pete, but I should be home each evening with my mother, and I'll certainly find time to visit my sisters.' He glanced at his companion. 'You're well? And Anneke?'

'Both well, I am happy to say, *mijnheer*. We hope that you will be here for some time.'

'Ten days, no longer.'

'You will perhaps spend more time in Holland when you are married?'

'My fiancée isn't keen on the idea, Pete. I must bring her over for a few days to meet the family.'

Pete remained silent. He had been with the family since Mr van Linssen was a little boy, running the household while his wife did the housekeeping, and after so many years in the family service he was regarded as a friend. After a few moments he said, 'She could not be anything but happy to live here, so quiet and peaceful by the lake, and yet so near Amsterdam and Utrecht.'

Mr van Linssen had driven the short distance south to Aalsmeer and turned on to the Hilversum road, but some six miles before he reached that city he turned into a country road running between the lakes which stretched for some miles on either side of it. It was pleasant country, giving one no inkling of the nearness of Hilversum and Utrecht, with trees bordering the road, pleasant villas at the water's edge, and from time to time a village. He was going south now towards Utrecht, but only for a short distance before he turned between brick pillars into a short drive and stopped before the house at its end.

It was a solid house, built of rose-coloured bricks, with a gabled roof and a great many windows. Those on the ground floor were tall and wide, but the nearer the roof the smaller they became, with leaded panes and painted shutters. He got out of the car and went up the double steps to the canopied front door while Pete got his bags from the boot. The door opened at his touch and he went inside to the wide hall, with its panelled walls and high plastered ceiling, and was met by a very small, very thin woman with brown hair, barely streaked with grey, and brown eyes. She burst into voluble Dutch, wringing his hand and then smiling broadly as he bent to kiss her cheek.

'Anneke, it's good to see you again.'

'You are alone?' she wanted to know. 'The young lady is not with you? We had hoped to see her...'

'Not this time, Anneke. Is my mother in the drawing-room?'

'Yes, and waiting for you. I will bring coffee, and presently there is a good supper for you.'

'Good, I'm famished.' He smiled at her and crossed the hall to open the double doors at one side and go into the room beyond.

His mother came to meet him as he went in, a tall woman with silver hair worn in an old-fashioned style, framing an elderly face which must at one time have been beautiful. Her eyes were blue and just now they were alight with pleasure. 'Fenno, my dear, this is delightful. You did not mind that I came here before you had arrived? I wish to see as much of you as possible and I know you will be away for most of your day.'

He kissed her cheek. 'Mama, there is nothing I could wish for more but to find you here waiting for me. I hardly saw you when I was last in Holland.'

'You are alone? You have not brought your fiancée with you?'

He answered her briefly. 'No, she did not wish to come.'

His mother gave him a sharp glance. 'Of course, it would be dull for her as you will be away for so much of the time.' She smiled at him. 'I must wait until the wedding, perhaps?'

His 'Perhaps' was uttered casually as he went to open the doors into the grounds at the back, to be greeted by the dog who came bounding in at his whistle.

Anneke came in then, with coffee and the information that supper would be served in twenty minutes or so. 'You waited for me?' he asked his mother.

'Yes, dear, you may well be gone in the morning by the time I get down, and probably you will be too tired to talk much in the evening. Will you be operating?'

'Yes, at Leiden. I shall be there for three days and then I go to Utrecht and finally to Amsterdam. You will stay?'

'Willingly, Fenno.' She spoke readily but she searched his face anxiously. She understood him very well: reserved to the point of coldness, generous to a fault, a steadfast friend, a compassionate man towards his patients and, hidden away beneath his beautiful manners, a romantic. Now there was something wrong, and most likely something to do with this Ursula he intended to marry. Even though she had never met her, Mevrouw van Linssen had taken a dislike to her; she had sent excuses for not accompanying Fenno on several occasions now, and it was obvious that she had no wish to meet his family. She began to talk about his younger sister who had just had a second son, and presently, when they had supper together, she gave him a light-hearted account of his friends' and family's doings since he had been away.

It wasn't until the following evening as they sat before the fire in the drawing-room, the dog at their feet, that he told her about Peter.

'He sounds a nice child,' said his mother, and hoped for more. Into the companionable silence she asked, 'You say he's an orphan, poor boy. I suppose his lives with his grandparents?'

'No, a cousin, and an old housekeeper.'

More promising, reflected Mevrouw van Linssen. 'How dull for him—I hope he has lots of friends.'

'Not dull at all. His cousin is in her late twenties.' He paused and she waited for more, but all he said was, 'The housekeeper worked for Eulalia's grandmother until she died. She had nowhere to go, so they made a home together, and then took on Peter when his parents were killed.'

He began to talk about something else, leaving his mother thoughtful.

He didn't speak of it again until the day before he was to return to England, when he was driving his mother back to her small town house in den Haag, and then in reply to her carefully careless question.

'See Peter? I doubt it. He lives in the Cotswolds. Besides, his cousin dislikes me.'

His voice was harsh, and she contented herself by saying casually, 'The Cotswolds are lovely, aren't they? All those charming houses.' But she thought to herself, so it is this aunt with the pretty name. Why didn't she like Fenno? She had no idea how to answer that question. Instead she begged him to give her love to Ursula. 'And do tell her that she must come and meet me before you marry,' a remark which he replied to with a grunt which could have meant anything.

The autumn days were shortening but the fine weather still held. Eulalia dug away at the garden, gradually reducing it to some kind of order, while old Bob, a bit too stiff for hard digging, saw to the fruit-trees and pruned anything that needed it. She had planted as she cleared, and already there were neat rows of winter cabbage, spinach, beet and turnips. It was a bit late in the year to plant, but the soil was good and the garden sheltered. When she wasn't busy in the garden she helped with the chores and did the shopping if Trottie's feet were painful. She had half expected to see Victor, but there was no sign of him. Mr van Linssen's bit of play-acting had frightened him off, and after a few days she stopped looking over her shoulder each time anyone went past the cottage, and on the following Sunday, although he was in church, sitting in his family pew, he avoided looking at her.

Trottie, who had been there too, remarked on that as they walked home with Peter between them. 'Depend on it, Miss Lally, he had a nasty fright; Mr van Linssen being such a big gentleman and with such a cold eye when it suits him. Happen that Victor thinks you're promised."

Eulalia tried to look unconcerned and blushed instead, so that Peter wanted to know why she had got so red. 'And why does Victor think you're promised?' he enquired. 'And what does that mean?'

Eulalia had always done her best to be a good guardian and that meant telling the truth as much as possible when he asked awkward questions. 'It's a rather old-fashioned way of saying you're engaged.'

Peter gave a little skip. 'To Mr van Linssen? How absolutely super. He'll be my cousin too, won't he?'

'No, dear, I must explain. He—just pretended, so that Victor would stop bothering me. He's going to marry Miss Kendall. He was just doing a kind act.'

She couldn't bear to see Peter's disappointed face. 'Never mind, love, I'm on the look-out for a millionaire who'll look after all of us forever and ever!'

'Oh, well,' said Peter. 'I suppose he'll do if we can't have Mr van Linssen.'

'Well, no, we can't,' agreed Eulalia, and felt unutterably sad at the thought.

Presently, when they had had their dinner and Peter was in the garden with Blossom and Charlie, and Trottie was having what she called her 'lay down', she brushed the sadness away; she had no reason to be sad about the man. They disagreed every time they met and he had a nasty knack of making her feel foolish. She was, of course, grateful to him, for he seemed to have a way of turning up at the right moment, but he was, she told herself, an arrogant man, given to sarcasm and with the gift of bringing out the worst in her. She would, she told herself resolutely, forget him.

It wasn't easy, but, the garden dealt with for the moment, she was able to turn her attention to plans for the shop. She had renewed old acquaintances by now and Peter had friends in the village. She went out to coffee-mornings, afternoons of tennis and the occasional dinner party, so that by the time she was ready to open the shop there would be a number of people who would come and buy flowers, out of curiosity at first and then, hopefully, because the shop and its contents were attractive. It would have to be just before Christmas, when she might hope to get orders for flower arrangements as well as cut flowers.

She spent her evenings making lists, planning how much money she dared spend and debating ways and means with Trottie. She intended to get Jacob to put up a small glasshouse attached to the bathroom wall, and get planning permission to knock a hole in the side wall of the garden and put a gate there, something she had discovered could be done since it wouldn't alter the appearance of the cottage. She still had to go and see Mr Willett and get his advice, and before that make a few tentative enquiries in the village to see what people thought of the idea. Not everyone, of course, but the rector, and old Colonel Grimes up at the Manor, and the doctor, and Mr Wedge at the Boy and Horseshoe...

She went one morning to see him first, leaving Peter with Trottie. It was mid-morning and there were only two people in the bar, while Mr Wedge leaned on his elbows, discussing politics. Eulalia, waiting until he had made short work of the government and politicians in general, finally asked for a cup of coffee. 'And if you could spare five minutes—I'd like your advice.'

'Lor', Miss Lally that's given for free, likewise the coffee. Trouble, is there?'

'No, no, Mr Wedge, just an idea I want to tell you about.'

The two men leaning on the bar came nearer. They were both elderly, long since retired from working on local farms and eager to hear what she had to say.

'You'm Miss Lally,' said the oldest man. 'I remember you when you was a little maid. Living in that Ivy Cottage that gentleman bought.' He turned to Mr Wedge. 'Remember, Tim? Him with that great big car. 'Ad it all cut and dried 'fore you could say knife. Wanted to know where that Mr Willett 'oo saw to Mrs Warburton's business, poor soul, lived. Mark you, 'e were a fool to buy the place. Leastways, it seemed so, but Miss Lally 'ere 'as done it up a treat.'

It took Eulalia a few moments to realise what the old man was saying. She went so pale that Mr Wedge cast her an anxious look, not sure what was wrong but sensing that something was amiss. He said, 'How about another half-pint, William, though you ought to be getting home or you'll have your missus after you.' It was a relief when William nodded reluctantly and made for the door with a cheerful 'See you' and a wave.

He was barely out of the door when Wedge said loudly, 'I'll fetch that cup of coffee, Miss Lally, now it's quiet. Tim here's a bit deaf so you can say what you want.'

Eulalia said slowly, 'If you don't mind, Mr Wedge, I'll come back later—I've just remembered something...' And she followed William out of the door. He was already halfway up the street but she caught up with him easily.

'May I walk a bit of the way with you? I want to ask you something?'

'Why not, missy? Time's me own when the wife's not badgering me.' He gave her a shrewd glance. 'Something I said back there in the pub?'

'Yes, the gentleman who bought Ivy Cottage. Did he give his name, was he English?'

'Didn't give no name, not to me, anyway. As for being a foreigner I wouldn't know. Spoke the Queen's English a sight better than me. Quiet kind of man and 'andsome. Pots of money, no doubt, with that car. It were a Bentley motor car, like Sir Percy over at Bowle House drives.' He stopped and took a look at her. 'Know 'im, do you, Miss Lally?'

'Oh, yes,' said Eulalia, in a voice which boded ill for Mr van Linssen, 'I know him.'

She bade him goodbye presently and walked back to Ivy Cottage, going at a great pace, propelled by rage. Trottie looked up from her knitting as she went in. 'And what's upset you, Miss Lally? Don't tell me it's that Victor...'

Eulalia stood in the centre of the little room, magnificent in her rage. She said between her teeth, 'Not Victor. Mr van Linssen. How dare he?'

Trottie put down her knitting. 'Well, tell old Trottie all about it,' she invited.

'This cottage—he bought it. William Thorpe told me, at least, he was talking to Wedge and I asked him.' She gave a great heaving breath. 'Don't you see, Trottie, it belongs to him? There's something fishy about that; he's played a trick on me.' She stopped to think. 'Do you suppose that he bought it from that great-uncle in Australia? No, of course he couldn't, and besides, I've got the deeds. I don't understand.'

Trottie knitted half a row. 'You'd best go and see that Mr Willett. He'll have the answer, I've no doubt.' She finished the row. 'That old William's getting on a bit, doesn't always know what he's talking about.'

Eulalia said doubtfully, 'Yes, perhaps that's it. All the same, I'm going to take the deeds and catch the bus into Cirencester this afternoon.'

'You do that,' advised Trottie. 'Don't go blaming that nice Mr van Linssen until you know he's guilty.'

'If he is, I'll never speak to him again.'

'Well, you're not likely to see him, are you, love?' said Trottie briskly. She folded up her knitting. 'I'll get us a bite to eat and you go and tidy yourself. You can't go to Cirencester in that old dress.'

It was mid-afternoon by the time Eulalia arrived at Mr Willett's office and requested his clerk for a few minutes of his time. She didn't have to wait long. Mr Willett came out of his room to meet her, shook hands in the most friendly fashion and ushered her in. He had seen her white face and eyes dark with rage, and embarked most prudently upon a series of questions as to her health, the health of Miss Trott, the well-being of Peter and a lengthy observation concerning the pleasure of living in a village again after the drabness of the Cromwell Road.

Eulalia replied politely and waited until he paused for breath.

'Did you know,' she asked without preamble, 'that Mr van Linssen had bought Ivy Cottage? And what about the money—all that money? And was there a great-uncle in Australia?'

Mr Willett sat back, his hands before him in an attitude of prayer, and looked grave. 'First, will you tell me from whom you have heard all this?'

So Eulalia took a calming breath and told him, and then sat waiting for him to answer.

'It is not within my power to discuss this matter with you, Eulalia. You must understand that. I am not at liberty to disclose my clients' private affairs.'

'That's absurd—however am I to find out the truth if someone doesn't tell me?'

Mr Willett switched on his intercom and requested two cups of tea. 'I can but advise you. Since you are anxious to solve the matter, I suggest that you should write to Mr van Linssen and put the matter before him.'

The tea came and she sipped it while she thought. 'But you did know about it?' she wanted to know.

Mr Willett nibbled a biscuit. 'My dear Eulalia, I have already told you that I am not in a position to reveal such information.'

'He was your client, though?' said Eulalia. She got no reply other than an offer of a second cup of tea. She liked Mr Willett, who had done his best for her when her grandmother had died, and now she said, 'All right, I'll write to him and see what he says. Thank you for your advice.' She got up. 'I'll let you know about his reply.'

He escorted her to the door and shook hands. 'I'm sure it can be settled,' he assured her. 'Some misunderstanding!'

He went back to his office and sat down to think. His first impulse was to telephone Mr van Linssen and tell him what had occurred, but on second thoughts he decided against it. He suspected that Mr van Linssen had more than an ordinary interest in Eulalia and who was he to interfere?

As for Eulalia, she went back to Ivy Cottage, assured Peter, back from school, that she had gone to see Mr Willett about a trifling matter, and remarked to Trottie that it had been very pleasant in Cirencester but the days were getting rather chilly, and after their supper she helped Peter with his homework and saw him into bed, accompanied by Charlie and Blossom. Only when he was asleep did she sit down and tell Trottie what Mr Willett had said. 'I'm going up to London tomorrow morning,' she declared. 'If I catch an early train I can be there by eleven o'clock. I'll go to Maude's and find out if he's there, and if he isn't I'll go to his house and wait for him.'

'Supposing he does own this house and the money too, what will you do, Miss Lally? You can give him back almost all the money, but you can't give him back this place, leastways, if you do, we'd be out in the street. And Peter? I know his school fees are safe but he's got to live somewhere, hasn't he? And him so happy with the garden and Charlie and Blossom?'

'I thought about that on my way home, Trottie. I'll pay back the money I haven't spent and I'll get work, any work, so's we can go on living here, and I'll pay the rent. In that way we are not beholden to him.' She swallowed back tears. 'Oh, why did he do it?'

Trottie had her own ideas about that but she didn't say anything, only remarked presently that that seemed a sensible thing to do and what kind of job had Eulalia in mind?

'Anything—in a supermarket? I shouldn't think you need qualifications for that—only references—or in a café or a restaurant.' She looked at her old friend. 'I'm so sorry, Trottie—all those dreams...'

'At least we're out of London, love, you're young and strong and Peter's happy, and I'm content like I never was in Cromwell Road.'

Eulalia gave her a hug. 'You're an angel. I'll make us a hot drink and we'll go to bed.'

She told Peter at breakfast that she was going to London for the day. 'A bit of business, nothing to worry over. I'll bring you back a *Beano* from the bookstall.'

'Oh, thanks, Aunt Lally, and will you have time to see Mr van Linssen?'

She wasn't going to lie to him. 'Darling, I don't know where he is, he might be in Holland, but if I do see him—and that's not likely, is it?—I'll give him your love.'

As soon as she had taken him to school she caught her bus and then the train, had a cup of coffee at the station buffet and caught a bus going west which would take her almost to Maude's Hospital. All the way there she had rehearsed what she would say; she would be quiet and cool and businesslike. She had, she honestly thought, bottled up her rage and humiliation; she would guard her tongue and not answer him back, however infuriating he became. She realised that if it was a misunderstanding she was open to his ridicule, but that was a small risk.

She got off the bus and went along to the entrance of the hospital and enquired of the porter if Mr van Linssen was there. The head porter looked at her most suspiciously. 'Patient, are you? You're in the wrong door, miss, and his clinic isn't till one o'clock. Better come back in an hour or so and go to the outpatients' door round to the right as you go out.'

He turned to answer the phone and she went out into the forecourt again. She was in luck. She would join the patients for his clinic; he would have to see her then. It meant that she would have to catch an evening train back home and probably miss the last bus to the village, but she could get a taxi.

She wasn't far from the park and there was a small café near there where she could get a sandwich and some coffee. The walk did her good, and she sat for half an hour eating her small meal before going into the park and walking briskly along its paths. It was a fine autumn day but there was a nip in the air, and she wished she had worn something warmer. Her jersey dress and jacket looked good, and to boost her self-confidence she had worn a hat, a small-brimmed velvet one, years old but dateless. She wasn't sure why she had taken such care with her clothes, perhaps to impress upon Mr van Linssen that she wasn't penniless and didn't need his charity. She even went over her speech again as she walked, and presently made her way back to the hospital and walked boldly into the outpatients' hall. It was crowded, which suited her very well, and there were notices on the wall pointing out where the patients for the various clinics should sit. Mr van Linssen's benches were already almost full when she approached them, to be halted by a fussy little woman who asked for her card.

Eulalia gave her her brightest smile. 'I'm not a patient. I have to see Mr van Linssen on a private matter and I haven't time to go to his home. May I sit here and see him when his patients have been attended to?'

The little lady pursed her lips. 'It's most unusual. I don't know what Sister will say.'

'If I'm not a patient, surely she need not be bothered,' Eulalia pointed out.

'That's true. You are personally acquainted with Mr van Linssen?'

'Oh, yes. Over a period of some months. He is a friend of my cousin.'

'Oh, well, I dare say that's all right. Sit on the far side of the back row. You'll have to wait a while—he's got a very full clinic today.'

Eulalia sat down where she was told and looked around her. A sister was bustling to and fro, so were several nurses, and presently two young housemen crossed the hall and went through a door close to the front bench, followed almost at once by a woman in a white overall with a great many papers under her arm, and five minutes later there was a wave of shuffling and head-turning and Mr van Linssen, looking quite different in his long white coat, crossed the hall. He was talking to a younger man and didn't look at anyone. She watched his massive back disappear through the door and felt a pang of something. Panic? Fear at having to face him? Pleasure at seeing him again? She didn't pursue the thought.

The next three and a half hours seemed endless. She longed for a cup of tea but she didn't dare leave her seat in case he went away. The benches slowly emptied, few remaining patients were in the hall now, and very soon she would get her chance. She went over her prepared speeches once more and, as the last patient was called in, moved to the front bench.

The man came out again in ten minutes, followed by the two housemen, a nurse and the older man with Sister. That lady pulled up short when she saw Eulalia. 'You're very late. Where are your notes? I doubt if Mr van Linssen will see you.'

Eulalia had slipped past her. 'I'm not a patient but I have to see him before he leaves.' She closed the door in Sister's astonished face and stood looking at Mr van Linssen, writing busily at his desk.

He didn't look up. 'Sister, we'll admit that last man...' He did look up then. His blue eyes, suddenly alert and cold, studied her for a moment, then he got slowly to his feet.

'Oh dear, oh dear,' said Mr van Linssen, and gave her a mocking smile which tore to shreds all her coolness and calmness and dignity and reduced her speeches to utter nonsense.

CHAPTER SEVEN

HE CAME forward and offered her a chair. 'Do sit down. I can see that you are bursting with the wish to give vent to your rage and to hurl abuse at my head.' He glanced at his watch. 'I can spare you ten minutes.'

Eulalia found her voice. It was rather shrill and not quite steady but she knew what she wanted to say. 'I do not care whether you can spare the time for me. I shall say what I have come to say, and if it takes more time than ten minutes, that's just too bad.'

He eyed her with appreciation; bad temper suited her. Her lovely grey eyes flashed, her cheeks were delightfully pink. She sat down deliberately, put her handbag on the floor and folded her hands on her lap. He saw that they were shaking and her charming bosom was heaving in a beguiling manner, and he sat back in his chair. He had been taken by surprise but he rather thought he was going to enjoy the next half-hour.

He said, as politely impersonal as a doctor to his patient, 'I'm listening, Eulalia.'

'Don't call me Eulalia,' she snapped.

'You shouldn't say that. I might be tempted to call you something else.'

'Oh, be quiet, do,' she snapped. Her carefully rehearsed speeches had flown out of her head. 'You tricked me, didn't you? There wasn't an uncle in Australia—how did you get Mr Willett to agree? And why did you do it?'

She paused, and he said smoothly, 'You are so sure that I have done this, but you have no proof. You may be mistaken, in which case your journey here, rather gratifying though it may be to myself, has been a waste of time and money.'

She stared at him, suddenly uncertain, and then remembered William.

'I have proof. William told me—he's an old man who lives in the village. He was in Wedge's bar when you were there. He remembered you because you had a Bentley motor car.'

Mr van Linssen laughed. 'How very lowering for my ego. Now that you have proof, what do you intend to do about it, Eulalia?'

'Give it all back, of course. I can't do that all at once, but I haven't used much of the money, and what I have used I'll pay back if it takes me the rest of my life. And we'll leave the cottage...'

His slow smile mocked her. 'Yes? And where will you go?'

'I'll find somewhere. I'm not a fool.'

'No, but pig-headed in the extreme. Come down off your high horse and use some sense. What about Peter and Miss Trott? Are they to suffer a homeless plight with you?'

He was sitting back in his chair, very much at his ease, and she felt rage bubbling up inside her again. She said in a cold voice with only the faintest quiver in it, 'I am not pig-headed.'

'No, no, of course not—a slip of the tongue. Let us say rather that you are a strong-minded female who likes her own way.'

The interview which she had planned so carefully had now become a fiasco and it was all his fault. Somehow she had been made to feel guilty. She sat silent, trying to regain her composure, not helped by him glancing at the watch he took from his waistcoat pocket.

'You are returning this evening to Brokenwell?'

'Yes.' She got up. 'There's no point talking to you. I'll go and see Mr Willett. I'll send you a cheque, and perhaps you would be good enough to tell me what rent you require?'

All he said was, 'You've missed your train. When is the next one?'

'Eight o'clock.'

'You won't be home until nearly midnight. Sit down, Eulalia.'

So she sat down again, quite glad to do so, for she was hungry and her feelings had left her tired and somewhat dispirited. Just for a moment she didn't care what was to happen next.

Mr van Linssen lifted the receiver and dialled. 'Dodge, will you go to the study and look in the phone book for the Boy and Horseshoe at Brokenwell and let me have the number?' In a few moments he said, 'Thank you,' and put down the receiver, to pick it up again and dial once more. 'Mr Wedge? Van Linssen here. Would you be good enough to send a message to Miss Trott at Ivy Cottage? Tell her that Miss Warburton will be staying as my guest until tomorrow morning and will return home some time during the day. Many thanks.'

He put the receiver down and Eulalia gasped, 'You can't do that...'

'I just have,' he pointed out in a reasonable voice, and sat back again, watching her.

Eulalia drew a long breath. She said in a voice that was getting rather shrill, 'I do not care for your arrangements, Mr van Linssen, I intend to go home.'

She got to her feet again and this time he did the same. 'Yes, yes.' He sounded impatient. 'But since I owe it to Miss Trott and Peter to return you safely to Brokenwell, you have no alternative but to do as I say.'

'You are an abominable man,' said Eulalia loudly, 'and I dislike you. I dislike you even more than I do Victor. You are high-handed and sarcastic and—and unkind, and if I had that money with me now I'd throw it at you, and the cottage as well.'

The absurdity of this remark didn't strike her, and whatever Mr van Linssen thought about it remained concealed by a perfectly expressionless face. He picked up the phone once more and spoke into it. 'Geoff? I've been called away. Will you collect the notes from Outpatients? I'll see to them later. Yes, in an hour or two.'

That done, he took Eulalia's arm and walked her briskly out of the room and across the hall and into the forecourt, bidding a surprised nurse and a porter goodnight as he went.

Eulalia went silently. There was a great deal she wanted to say, but she was so angry that her thoughts weren't making sense, and putting them into words would be useless. She sat beside him in the car, as still and stiff as a poker, her lovely nose in the air, vexed even more by Mr van Linssen's casual manner. He could have been delivering a parcel for all the notice he took of her.

She said suddenly, 'I am doing this against my will and I protest very strongly.'

'Don't be so silly,' observed Mr van Linssen in a voice to dampen down even the strongest feelings.

That was the extent of their conversation until they reached his house.

Dodge, advancing to meet them as they went in, showed no surprise, but inclined his head gravely and bade her good evening and stood listening to his master telling him to take Miss Warburton to the guest-room so that she might tidy herself.

'Miss Warburton has missed her train. She will spend the night here and return to Brokenwell in the morning. Could we have a tray of tea in ten minutes or so, and dinner at the usual hour? See that Miss Warburton has all she wants, will you?'

He turned to Eulalia. 'Do come down when you're ready. I'm sure you would like a cup of tea. The cure for all ills in this country, is it not?'

He waited until she had followed Dodge upstairs, and then went along to his study to let his registrar know that he would be back at Maude's in a couple of hours.

Eulalia was ushered into a charming room at the back of the house, overlooking the tiny garden beyond which there was a narrow road and on the other side of it a row of mews cottages. She looked out of the window and then turned to survey the room. It was quite small but most elegantly furnished, with a peach silk bedspread and curtains, a satinwood dressing-table and two small easy chairs and a thick cream-coloured carpet, and when she peered round a door beside the bed she discovered a bathroom, equipped with thick peach-coloured towels, soap, powder, bath essence... There was even a toothbrush and hairbrush and comb.

Perhaps Ursula comes here, thought Eulalia, unaware that it was Dodge's pride that unexpected guests would find everything they could need.

She poked at her hair, powdered her nose, applied lipstick and went downstairs, outwardly serene, inwardly quaking.

The drawing-room was as beautiful as she had remembered, more so now perhaps, since there was a bright fire in the steel grate and a small table had been drawn up to it on which was a silver teapot and delicate cups and saucers and a plate of fairy-cakes. Mr van Linssen drew a chair forward for her and asked her to pour out in a no-nonsense voice, and sat down again in a vast wing-chair. It was all very cosy and domestic, made more so by the presence of Mabel, curled up before the fire. It was all so normal, too, thought Eulalia. It seemed right that they should be sitting there facing each other, drinking their tea and eating Dodge's delicious little cakes. She gave herself a mental shake. She mustn't allow herself to be soothed; Mr van Linssen would take advantage of that and make some preposterous suggestion about the cottage and all that money...

He did no such thing, however, merely made absent-minded conversation, offered the cakes, had a second cup of tea, and then excused himself with the plea that he had some telephoning to do, leaving her with Mabel for company and a pile of newspapers.

She put these down presently and got up and wandered round the room, examining the pictures and the books housed in the handsome breakfront Georgian bookcase. They were handsomely bound, probably first editions, she thought, and some of them had titles in what she supposed was Dutch. She walked to the window and stood looking out into the already darkening evening. It was quiet, and she thought it was almost as peaceful as Brokenwell. She was still standing there when Mr van Linssen came back, offered her a drink and, when she had sat down, went to his chair again.

She answered his remarks with polite brevity, although this didn't appear to discompose him in the least, for he made easy conversation until Dodge came to tell them that dinner was served.

Eulalia, whose insides were hollow with hunger, was sensible enough to polish off lobster bisque, chicken à la king and chocolate pudding, as light as air and smothered in cream. It made no difference, she told herself, that she was at the table of a man she disliked; she had been famished and it was good sense to eat a meal, even though she sat unwillingly at his table. Mindful of her manners and swallowing her temper with the soup, she replied suitably to her companion's casual talk and had a second helping of pudding. They had their coffee at the table and, as soon as they had drunk it, Mr van Linssen got up.

'You'll forgive me if I leave you in Dodge's care? I have to return to Maude's and I may be back late. If I don't see you in the morning, tell him which train you wish to catch and he will see you on your way.'

He didn't wait for her answer but gave her a curt 'Goodnight' over his shoulder as he left the dining-room, and a moment later she heard the front door close. It was strange, she reflected, that she should feel lonely the moment he was out of the house.

Dodge ushered her back into the drawing-room, offered magazines, switched on the television set concealed in a corner of the room, and indicated that suitable night-things had been put in her room for her use.

'Early-morning tea at half-past seven, miss, if that is agreeable to you?'

'Yes—yes, thank you. I should like to catch the ten-forty train.'

'Certainly, miss. If there is something else you require, just ring the bell by the fireplace.'

'I think I'll go to bed early...'

'In that case, I wish you goodnight, miss. I trust you will sleep well.'

She thought it unlikely; there was too much on her mind. She had a long hot bath, doing sums in her head, calculating to the last penny how much she could pay back at once, and there was the rent...

She got into bed wearing the silk and lace nightie she had found draped over a chair. Whose? she wondered as she put it on, and then forgot about it as she climbed into bed and settled against the pillows. She still had a lot of thinking to do—she switched off the bedside lamp and lay in the dark. What was she going to tell Peter? She was asleep before she had the answer.

She woke to find a stout woman in a print overall arranging a small tray of tea by the bed. She drew back the curtains and wished Eulalia good morning in a cheerful cockney voice, adding, 'Breakfast in half an hour, miss,' and went away.

Eulalia sat up in bed and drank her tea and ate the wafer-thin slices of bread and butter. There was a lot to be said for luxury; she only hoped that Mr van Linssen's Ursula appreciated the prospect of a comfortable future. She had a shower, dressed, and went downstairs, torn between the hope that Mr van Linssen would be there and a wish never to set eyes on him again.

He was there at the breakfast-table in a charming little room at the back of the house. He got up as she went in, wished her good morning with impersonal politeness, expressed the hope that she had slept well and invited her to sit down. So she sat, poured her coffee, accepted the offer of scrambled eggs from Dodge and started her meal, turning over in her mind suitable topics for conversation. Never mind that she detested the sight of him sitting there so handsome and self-assured, good manners demanded that. While she was still formulating a remark about the weather, he got to his feet again. 'You will forgive me? I have an early appointment. Dodge will see you safely away.'

'Oh—I'll write—no, I won't. Mr Willett can write about paying back the money and the rent and...'

He said with barely concealed impatience, 'Yes, yes, do whatever you wish. Please give my regards to Miss Trott and my warmest greetings to Peter.'

'He asked me to give you his love.' She saw him glance at his watch and hurried on. 'And thank you for your hospitality, you have been most kind.'

His smile mocked her. 'You're too old to tell fibs,' he observed and went away, closing the door gently behind him.

She finished her breakfast, her thoughts in a fine muddle, and Dodge came presently to tell her that he would drive her to the station in good time to catch her train.

'There's really no need. I can get a bus and I'll leave with time to spare.'

'We have a small car for use in town, miss. Mr van Linssen asked me to see you safely on to your train.'

His look was so reproachful that she gave in.

The small car turned out to be a beautifully kept Rover. Still looking melancholy, Dodge drove through the traffic, parked the car and accompanied her on to the platform, pausing on the way to purchase a couple of newspapers and a magazine or two which he handed to her as she got into the train. She thanked him and shook his hand and he gave her a rare smile.

'I wish you a safe journey, miss, and hope to see you again.'

'Thank you, Dodge. I don't expect to come to London again. Thank you for making me so comfortable.'

He stood on the platform as the train drew away. His mournful expression didn't reflect his thoughts. She would be back if the master had anything to do with it. He dismissed Miss Kendall without a second thought—she hadn't a chance against this nice young lady...

Eulalia got back to Ivy Cottage in time to share her lunch with Trottie, and that lady, taking one look at her downcast face, said comfortably, 'No need to talk for the moment, Miss Lally, take off that jacket and sit down. I've some pasties in the oven and a cup of tea to wash them down.'

Over their second cup of tea Trottie observed mildly, 'That was kind of Mr van Linssen to send a message and look after you for the night. I was getting that uneasy.'

Eulalia put down her cup. 'I went to the hospital and saw him there. He—he found it amusing that I had found out about the cottage and all that money. He didn't make any excuse or give a reason—he called me pig-headed. I wish I had thrown something at him...'

'You always were an impetuous girl,' said Trottie. 'You came to some agreement?'

'Yes—no. I don't know, he just didn't care. I said I'd see Mr Willett and send back as much money as I had and pay rent for this cottage. He wasn't a bit interested,' she added crossly. 'He practically ordered me to spend the night at his house.'

'Well, love, London's a nasty place after dark for young women on their own. He did quite right.' She glanced at Eulalia's unhappy face. 'You won't be seeing him again?'

'Certainly not. Besides, he has no reason to come here.'

Trottie could think of a very good reason but she didn't say so. Mr van Linssen was old and wise enough to arrange his life to his own satisfaction. As for Lally, once she had simmered down and thought things over... Trottie, an incurable romantic, nodded to herself.

Eulalia said thoughtfully, 'I don't need to tell Peter anything, do I? I won't be able to open the shop this year. I'll get a job. It'll have to be part-time so that I can fit in the buses... I can tell him that I've decided to learn a bit more about it before starting on my own. Could we manage, Trottie?'

'Of course we can, Miss Lally. We'll have all the veg and fruit we need—we can splash out a bit at weekends when he's home.' She added bracingly, 'It's a sight better than Cromwell Road.'

'Oh, Trottie, I know, only I feel humiliated; he was amused, just as though it was a joke. I felt like someone to whom he's thrown money in the street.'

'Now, now, Miss Lally, you didn't ought to think that. He's a good man, only he don't let it show.'

'I hate him,' said Eulalia fierily.

All the same, she presented her usual serene face when Peter came back from school, gave him a suitably expurgated version of her visit to London, added Mr van Linssen's greetings and answered his eager questions as to how he had looked and what he had said.

He asked wistfully, 'He didn't say he'd come and see me?'

'Well, no, darling. He leads such a busy life. When he took me to his house yesterday evening he only stayed a little while, because he had to go back to the hospital, and in the morning when I went down to breakfast he had to go within a few minutes.'

'When he marries,' said Peter, 'his wife and children won't see him very often, will they?'

She had a quick mental picture of him sitting at the head of his breakfast-table with a smiling wife facing him and children on either side of him—several children, she reflected, he was a man to want a family. She shook the thought away; if he married his Ursula he would be lucky to have one lonely child, and he or she would probably be out of sight in the nursery. She felt a sudden pang of pity for him. She must stop thinking about him, and when she did, it must be with dislike.

Her pity was wasted, of course. Mr van Linssen needed none; he was in complete command of his destiny, even though it would need some rearranging before it was to his liking. Even the arrival of Ursula on the following evening did nothing to destroy his calm.

She brushed past Dodge as though he wasn't there and flung into the dining-room where Mr van Linssen was eating his dinner.

'Where were you last night?' she demanded. 'Dulcie Shaw saw you in the car with a girl. Who was she and why was she with you?'

He put down his napkin and got to his feet. 'My dear Ursula, this is an unexpected pleasure. You won't mind if I finish dinner? I had no time for lunch today. Can Dodge bring you something?'

'I dined hours ago,' she snapped, 'at the Shaws'—Dulcie was there, of course, sniggering about it. You should have been with me...'

Mr van Linssen selected cheese and took a biscuit. 'My dear Ursula, I seem to remember that you refused my invitation to the theatre yesterday evening on the grounds that you would be bored and would much prefer the Shaws' company.'

'That's quite different. It's a boring play, from all accounts, and why should I have to spend a tedious evening when I might be having fun?'

'Why, indeed? Do you find me tedious, Ursula?' He was watching her under lowered lids.

She pouted and said in a wheedling tone, 'Well, you are rather dull, darling. You still haven't told me who she was.'

'I don't intend to tell you, Ursula. Shall we go to the drawing-room for coffee?'

Her face became ugly with temper. 'I'm going, and I hope you'll be sorry for being so beastly to me—and don't think you can get round me with a stupid bunch of flowers.'

She flounced into the hall, and Dodge, looking suitably grieved, opened the door for her and bade her goodnight in a doleful voice before going off to his kitchen, where he fell to whistling cheerfully while he collected the plates and cutlery ready for the daily woman to clean when she came in in the morning. Very satisfactory, he decided. Now it only needed a bit of luck...

Which, as it turned out, was by no means as unlikely at it seemed. It was a Saturday afternoon and Trottie and Peter had gone to the village shop, leaving Eulalia at home, writing careful answers to the offers of work in the local weekly paper. They didn't intend to buy much: a tin of corned beef—Trottie was clever at serving it up in a hundred and one different guises—dog food, cat food and, since it was the weekend, Peter had his pocket-money to spend. Fifty pence a week wasn't much but he

laid it out carefully, and Mrs Trusk, who owned the shop,
allowed him to take his time deciding between fruit-gums
and humbugs. She wasn't busy, anyway, and she and
Trottie had plenty to gossip about.

He made his choice, and Trottie moved away from
the counter, caught her foot on the corner of a box of
oranges and fell. She was a stout little person and fell
hard. Peter had rushed to help her up but she put out
a shaking hand. 'No, love—leave me—I've hurt my leg.'
She gave him a lop-sided smile and fainted.

Mrs Trusk, bending over Trottie, said unnecessarily,
'She's fainted. Oh, dear, whatever shall we do?'

'Ring the doctor,' said Peter, 'and get a glass of water.'
He picked up one of Trottie's hands. 'Trottie—it's all
right, we'll look after you.'

His voice quavered a bit; he was, after all, only eight
years old, despite his efforts to be calm, like his idol Mr
van Linssen.

Trottie opened her eyes. 'I know you will, ducks—
don't let anyone move me.'

The doctor was on his rounds and his wife didn't know
where exactly. By then several people had gathered
round. 'Ring the ambulance,' said Mr Wedge and then,
'Someone get a cushion for Miss Trott's head.' He looked
around him. 'And someone fetch Miss Lally.'

Peter slipped behind the counter again and went to
the phone. Glad that he had Mr van Linssen's phone
number, he dialled it, and when someone answered he
said in a rush, 'I must speak to Mr van Linssen, it's very
important. Tell him it's Peter.'

He sighed gustily when the well-remembered voice said
in his small ear, 'Peter, what's wrong? Can I help?'

'It's Trottie, she's fallen down and she can't get up
because of her leg and the doctor isn't here. They've

sent for an ambulance but it's got to come from Cirencester and someone's gone to fetch Aunt Lally...' He paused on an indrawn breath, determined not to cry but wanting to very badly.

'Good man. You did quite right to ring me. Now, listen very carefully. I am going to get into my car and drive to Cirencester. It so happens that I have a good friend there. He'll allow me to take a look at Trottie and do anything that's necessary. Lally will have to go with Trottie. I want you to find Mr Wedge and ask him to go with you to the cottage and stay there until I come. I shall have Dodge with me and he will stay with you as long as it is necessary. I should be with you in a couple of hours. There's no need to tell Lally; she has enough to worry about. Tell her you'll be quite all right until she gets home. Have you got all that, Peter?'

'Yes, Mr van Linssen. I knew you'd come.'

He put the receiver back and joined the group around Trottie. Eulalia was kneeling beside her now, holding her hand and talking to her in a quiet voice, and above the babel of voices was the raucous sing-song of the ambulance. Peter touched Eulalia on the arm. 'You'll go with Trottie?' he asked. 'I'll be all right until you get home.'

'But someone must stay with you.'

'I'll get Mr Wedge—I know he will.'

Eulalia nodded. 'That's splendid of you, Peter. Look, stay here with Trottie while I run back and get her overnight things. She may need to stay in hospital.' She gave his small shoulder a squeeze and darted away, and by the time the paramedics had Trottie on a stretcher, her leg tenderly encased in a plastic splint, she was back again.

'Go home with Mr Wedge, darling, and stay indoors. The key's on the hook. I should be back soon after tea, but you get a meal if you're hungry, and feed Blossom and Charlie.' She gave him a quick hug. 'Bless you, Peter.'

There was no time for more. He watched the ambulance drive away and then went home. Mr Wedge went with him, a comforting arm around his small shoulders. 'There's bound to be some news quite soon, and I'll stay just as long as I'm needed.'

The cottage was very quiet. Mr Wedge made some tea and cut some bread and butter. Peter, with his mouth full, explained about Dodge.

'Now that's a grand idea. Nice chap, is he, this Dodge?'

'Oh, yes, Mr Wedge. He looks after Mr van Linssen.'

Mr Wedge, his mind set at rest, poured the tea.

Dodge was in the kitchen, preparing a béchamel sauce with which to coat the chicken he was preparing for that evening's meal—to be served earlier than usual, since Mr van Linssen was to escort his Ursula to some late evening function or other. He was quite unprepared for his master's sudden appearance.

'Ah, Dodge. Leave everything, pack two overnight bags, one for me, one for you. Ten minutes—you can have ten minutes.'

'Sir,' said Dodge in a pained voice.

'Yes, yes. I'll explain as we go. Now hurry, there's a good chap.'

Something in Mr van Linssen's voice made him do exactly that; within ten minutes he was coming down the stairs at twice his usual stately pace, a bag in each hand. A minute later he was sitting beside Mr van Linssen, listening to that gentleman's quiet voice explaining. Dodge had never looked anything other than melancholy all his life but now he allowed himself a smile. Here was a bit of luck, unless he was mistaken.

'Miss Kendall,' he ventured. 'You were to attend a function with her.'

'Oh, lord, yes. Dodge, pick up the phone and ring her now. Tell her that I'm called away on an urgent case.'

Dodge listened unmoved to Ursula's cross voice, expressed his regret and put the phone back. After that they didn't speak. The motorway was fairly empty: the weekenders had already gone and the evening traffic wouldn't start up for another two or three hours. Mr van Linssen sped along the fast lane and Dodge prayed that there would be no police patrols about.

They were nearing Cirencester when Mr van Linssen finally spoke. 'Dodge, I'll drop you off at Ivy Cottage. See to the boy, won't you? Get a meal if it's needed. I'll probably drive Miss Warburton back later, when we know what the damage is.'

He turned off the motorway and took the road to Malmesbury, and presently drove slowly through Brokenwell and stopped at Ivy Cottage. They both got out and Peter saw them from the window, and the next moment he had unlocked the door. He said in a small voice, 'I knew you'd come,' and Mr van Linssen put a great arm around him and turned to shake Mr Wedge's hand.

'Many thanks. I'm grateful,' he said quietly, and then, to Peter, 'Well, of course, friends help friends, you know, and how splendid of you to know what to do. I've brought Dodge with me. He's going to stay here while I go and see how Trottie is. He'll stay here tonight too, so if I don't bring your aunt Lally back by bedtime, you go to bed as usual.'

Peter nodded. 'All right, but you'll tell me if anything's wrong?'

'At once. That's a promise. Now I'm off. *Tot ziens*.'

'What does that mean?' asked Peter, as he and Dodge went back into the cottage, after waving goodbye to him and to Mr Wedge.

'See you later,' said Dodge. 'Now, how about us doing some cooking when we've had a cup of tea? I'm a dab hand at it.'

Eulalia sat by Trottie in the ambulance, holding her hand. Trottie's face was pale and her eyes were closed, but now and again she opened her eyes and smiled. 'Silly me,' she whispered. 'Ought to know better at my age.'

Eulalia murmured in a comforting voice, 'Mrs Trusk leaves boxes all over the shop. Don't worry, Trottie, we'll have you home again in no time at all.'

At the hospital she was asked to wait while Trottie was examined. It seemed an age before a nurse came to tell her that she could sit with her for a while. 'She's been X-rayed,' the nurse explained, 'but we'll have to wait for a little while until they're looked at. She's a bit drowsy— she was given something for the pain.'

Trottie was half asleep. 'It don't hurt now,' she assured Eulalia. 'I'll be all right, Miss Lally, do you go home to Peter.'

'In a little while. He's quite all right, Mr Wedge said that he would stay with him. He'll know what to do. Don't worry, Trottie, everything's fine.'

Trottie dozed off and Eulalia sat holding her hand, thinking about the future. It would have to be replanned. She couldn't take a job until Trottie was fit again, and if it was a badly broken leg—and from the glimpse she had had of it when the paramedics had examined it, it certainly looked as if it was—then she would have to stay at home for some time. She couldn't work in the village even if there was work to be had, for everyone would want to know why she—possessed of her own cottage and a handsome bank balance—should need a job, and sooner or later Peter would hear of it . . .

A young doctor interrupted her thoughts, beckoning her away to tell her that Mr Wyatt, the consultant ortho-paedic surgeon, would like a word with her. She was led away to a small office and found him sitting at a desk and Casualty Sister standing beside him.

'Miss Warburton?' He shook hands. 'You must be anxious about Miss Trott. The X-rays show that the two lower bones of her left leg are broken. Rather nasty breaks, I'm afraid, which will need surgery. This will mean a stay in hospital while the wound heals. The leg will be put in plaster and there is no reason why she shouldn't return home once she has got used to crutches. She has every chance of recovering completely.'

'When will you operate?'

'Within the next hour or so. Miss Trott is shocked—a brief rest is to her advantage.'

'I'd like to stay until the operation is finished.'

'Of course. Would you like to stay with Miss Trott now for a while? When she goes to Theatre, Sister will show you where you can wait.'

She went back to Trottie, who was awake now and rather tearful.

'It's all right, Trottie,' said Eulalia. 'I've seen the surgeon. He's going to see to your leg very soon and I'll stay until you are back in bed.'

As she spoke she was vaguely aware that someone had come into the department. There was a rumble of voices, and a moment later the cubicle curtain was drawn aside and Mr van Linssen, looking as calm and at ease as though he had just got out of his armchair, came to stand by the couch.

He nodded at Eulalia, smiling a little at her open-mouthed astonishment, and then turned his attention to Trottie, who looked up at him and smiled.

'Now I'll be all right,' she said.

CHAPTER EIGHT

MR VAN LINSSEN took her hand in his. 'Of course you will. Mr Wyatt and I are going to have a look at that leg, and presently we'll put the bones together and give you a plaster.' He looked across at Eulalia.

'If Eulalia would wait somewhere while we are doing it...'

She bent and kissed Trottie's cheek, not looking at him. 'I'll see you later, Trottie, when you are back in your bed.'

He gave her a searching look as she went past him. 'Don't worry—such an easy thing to say, but I promise you Trottie will be as good as new.'

She nodded because she believed him. Even though she disliked him, she told herself, he had never lied to her.

There was no one else in the waiting-room. She leafed through the pile of old magazines and drank the tea a nurse brought her, and tried not to think about Trottie in Theatre now, with Mr van Linssen bending over her unconscious little body. She found to her shame that she was snivelling, and wiped her eyes and blew her nose in a vain effort to stop the tears. They went on trickling down her cheeks and presently she gave up mopping them. There was no one to see...

Mr van Linssen, still in his green theatre kit, his mask pulled down under his chin, loomed in the doorway. 'You had better mop your face,' said he cheerfully. 'Trottie

145

is already awake. If she sees you in tears she'll probably insist on going home.' He added, 'There's nothing to cry about, you know.'

Her hanky was sodden, and she wiped her eyes with the back of her hands like a child. 'I wish I knew the right words to tell you what I think of you,' she said in a watery voice, and then, remembering, 'But you've been very kind. I'm—I'm very grateful.'

'Yes, yes, leave the gratitude for the moment. Come and see Trottie.'

She got up then and went to the door. 'She's going to be all right? Was her leg very bad?'

'Nothing which couldn't be put right. I've set the bones and her leg is in plaster. Mr Wyatt will keep her here for a few days—I had to make a small incision in order to get the bones in alignment. Once the wound has closed she can come home. Come along, now.'

Trottie was in a small ward with half a dozen other patients, in a corner bed with the curtains still drawn round it. Mr van Linssen pulled them apart and gave Eulalia a small shove. 'You can have ten minutes,' he told her, and went away to where Sister was waiting for him at the other end of the ward.

Trottie was awake, nicely cushioned with pillows, her plastered leg under a cradle so that it would dry and allow the wound, visible through the little window cut in the plaster, to be inspected.

'I'm such a nuisance, Miss Lally.'

'Rubbish, Trottie. You've been marvellous. Mr van Linssen says you will be able to come home very soon and everything's fine. I'll be going home presently, but I'll come tomorrow with some more nighties for you. What about some books?'

'Just my knitting, love. Is Peter all right?'

'Yes. Mr Wedge is with him, and I'll be home in time to get his supper and get him to bed.' She saw Trottie's eyes close and bent and kissed her. 'Sleep well, Trottie, there's nothing to worry about.'

Trottie opened an eye. 'Well, of course not, with that dear man looking after us.' The eye closed, and in a few moments Eulalia left her.

Sister was in the ward talking to a nurse, but there was no sign of Mr van Linssen. Eulalia wondered why he had been there and supposed that he was called to any hospital which might need him. He was already on his way home, probably. Sister came to meet her.

'You'll be coming tomorrow? If you would bring a dressing-gown and more nighties—we shan't need to keep Miss Trott in for more than a few days, a week at the most. Come when you like in the afternoon or evening. Goodnight, Miss Warburton.'

Eulalia said goodnight and went slowly down the staircase. She would have to get a taxi to Brokenwell, for the last bus would have left by now. She stopped to count the money in her purse, afraid that she wouldn't have enough, and was interrupted by Mr van Linssen saying rather testily, 'Come along, Peter will be wondering what's happened to you...'

'You're still here...?'

'Well, of course I am. Now, do come along like a good girl. The car's on the other side of the forecourt.'

She hung back. 'I don't know how you got here,' she began. 'I mean, it was a surprise, but very lucky for Trottie, but you've taken care of her and there's no need to drive me home, it's out of your way.'

'Nothing of the sort. Dodge is with Peter and I fully expect that between them they will have got a meal for us.'

'Dodge?' asked Eulalia faintly. 'He's here too?'

She was thrust into the car without further ado and he got in beside her. 'Company for Peter.'

She turned to look at him as he drove away. 'I don't understand.'

'Peter had the good sense to phone me before the ambulance arrived.'

'Phone you?' She frowned. 'But we haven't got a phone. Besides...'

'The village shop has, and he used it.'

'And you came, just like that?'

'Yes.'

'But how did he know your phone number?'

'I gave it to him.'

She thought this over. 'Why?'

'Various reasons.' He had slowed the car and stopped outside the cottage, and its door was flung open at once and Peter came racing out.

'Is Trottie all right? Did you operate? Will you explain it to me later?' He beamed at Mr van Linssen and gave Eulalia a hug. 'You've been crying, your face is all blotchy.' He reached up to kiss her. 'Never mind, Aunt Lally, Mr Dodge has cooked a most gorgeous supper.'

Mr van Linssen was standing by the car watching them, and she said quickly, 'Please come in and have supper. You must be hungry, and I know Peter's dying to talk to you.'

He thanked her gravely, searching her face, and she turned away feeling shy all of a sudden, relieved to find Dodge standing just inside the door. He looked as downcast as usual as he greeted her. 'I have prepared a meal, miss, and I trust that you do not consider it presumption on my part. Young Peter has been of great assistance in its preparation.'

'How very thoughtful of you, Dodge. Supper would be lovely, and I'm sure Mr van Linssen is hungry.'

'Famished. Peter, if you'd like to sit here beside me I'll explain about Trottie while Eulalia tidies herself.'

'What you mean is,' said Eulalia very clearly, 'I must go and wash the tears from my face.' She glared at him, and went into the bathroom and stayed there for much longer than necessary, trying to regain her composure. When she went back into the kitchen, Dodge was dishing up and Mr van Linssen and Peter, heads together, were far too absorbed to notice her, or so she thought.

She offered to help Dodge, who accepted with dignity as he dished soup into the plates and removed a pie from the oven. 'I ventured to make sufficient pastry for a second pie, miss. I thought that you might like it for cold tomorrow. Steak and kidney with a trace of onion.'

'Did I have any steak and kidney in the house? I don't remember...'

'Peter and I visited the butcher, miss. He has excellent meat.'

Mr van Linssen had got up and was pouring sherry. 'Something smells delicious, Dodge. Have a glass of sherry before we start on it?'

'I haven't any sherry——' began Eulalia, and was interrupted by Dodge.

'We visited Mr Wedge, miss, in order to tell him that he had no more need to worry about Peter, and I, quite by chance, noticed a particularly good sherry there; a little stimulant is sometimes necessary.'

Mr van Linssen hid a smile and they drank their sherry and sat down to their supper.

The talk, naturally enough, was of Trottie. 'We'll fetch you directly after lunch tomorrow,' said Mr van Linssen. 'Trottie will be feeling quite herself by then and will no doubt be pleased to see visitors.'

Eulalia said quickly, 'There's no need—I mean, Peter and I can go, but you must want to return to London.'

'Certainly not. Pray don't deprive us of a day in the country. Dodge certainly deserves a day out, don't you, Dodge?'

'Indeed I do, sir, and I trust that I may have the opportunity of meeting Miss Trott—a lady of courage and spirit, I gather.'

Eulalia ate her soup and her pie and the crème brûlée Dodge had conjured up, and discovered that the future wasn't as black as she had thought it to be. Mr van Linssen had given her a detailed account of Trottie's injury and said confidently that there was no reason why she shouldn't be back and getting around with crutches in a very short time. 'And the sooner she is back pottering around the house the better. We'll have to change the plaster later on, and she'll need a quick check-up from time to time. That's no problem. I can drive down and see her here; there is no need for her to wait around at the hospital... I'll talk to Wyatt about that.'

'So you'll come again,' shrilled Peter happily.

'If Eulalia allows me to do so.'

He looked at her and gave her a small, mocking smile and she said coolly, 'Of course. You're very kind.' And because he was still smiling, she added, 'Peter, it's time you were in bed. You've had such a busy day and thank you for being so quick to help Trottie. I'm proud of you.'

'Well, Mr van Linssen wasn't here, so I had to get him, didn't I?'

He shook hands with Mr van Linssen, then with Dodge, and wanted to know if he had to have a bath.

'Have it in the morning, dear. I'll be up in two ticks to make sure you're in bed. Only clean your teeth.'

'While you're tucking him up, we'll wash up before we go.'

'Go? Not back to London?'

'No, no. Dodge, I feel sure, has booked rooms for us at Mr Wedge's.'

'Oh.' She stood uncertainly. 'I'm afraid I've not enough rooms here.'

'You have been most kind giving us supper.'

'Which Dodge cooked...'

'But you were not compelled to invite us.'

Peter came out of the bathroom then and she went upstairs with him, and when she came down again presently it was to find the washing-up done and Mr van Linssen arranging the spoons and forks tidily in their drawer while Dodge hung up the tea-towels. 'There was no need,' she began. 'You've both done all the work. Thank you.'

'Dodge is a dab hand at washing dishes, and I'm learning fast,' said Mr van Linssen. 'Goodnight, Eulalia.' He walked across the room to her, bent and kissed her, and went through the door, leaving her with her mouth open.

'Time for a nightcap before we go to bed,' observed Mr van Linssen to Dodge, and led the way down the street to the Boy and Horseshoe.

As for Eulalia, she stood for quite some time, doing nothing at all, trying to convince herself that she didn't like Mr van Linssen and having finally to admit that, despite his offhand manner and his tiresome habit of always being right, she liked him very much.

You can stop there, my girl, she told herself, he's all but a married man.

She went to bed presently, peeping into Peter's room to find him fast asleep with Charlie and Blossom curled up on the end of the bed. She thought of Mr van Linssen over at the Boy and Horseshoe and wondered if he was asleep too. It would be nice to see him tomorrow, she thought as she closed her eyes, but he shouldn't have kissed her. Not like that, for it hadn't been a social peck, far from it. And she had enjoyed it.

She and Peter went to church in the morning, then went back to eat Dodge's excellent pie before collecting such things as Trottie might want for the next few days, and that was barely done before the Bentley drew up before the door.

Mr van Linssen greeted them pleasantly, suggested that Charlie might go with them, settled the three of them in the back, waited patiently while Eulalia went back to make sure that Blossom was indoors, and with Dodge beside him drove to the hospital, where he persuaded Charlie to stay in the car and led his little party inside.

Trottie was sitting up in bed, looking small by reason of the cradle in the bed, but her colour had returned and her hair was brushed back into its usual severe bun. She beamed at them all and looked enquiringly at Dodge.

'Miss Trott, this is Mr Dodge, who runs my home for me.' Mr van Linssen smiled at them both in turn. 'I'm sure he'll want to tell you how much he likes Ivy Cottage.

Eulalia and I are going to talk to Sister for a few minutes. When we come back, Peter, I don't think anyone would mind if we took a look round together.'

He looked at Eulalia then, an unsmiling look, and she found herself blushing under it, quite unable to look away from him. She might have stood there for untold moments if Peter hadn't said, 'Do hurry, Aunt Lally, there's such a lot to see.'

She walked beside him as they went down the ward and into Sister's office, where they were joined by the young doctor who had first seen Trottie in Casualty. He eyed Eulalia with open admiration and treated Mr van Linssen with a respect which made her realise what an important man he was in his profession. Miss Trott was doing well, he assured him, and continued in technicalities, leaving her to listen to Sister's reassuring remarks about Trottie. Presently they went back to the ward and Peter skipped away with Mr van Linssen, while she sat down beside Trottie's bed and listened to Dodge discussing the best method with which to make choux pastry, his usually sombre face positively animated. She glanced at Trottie, whose cheeks were nicely pink. She was smiling at him while she contradicted him flatly, something he took in good part.

Back at the cottage, it seemed only polite to ask them in for a cup of tea, an offer which Mr van Linssen accepted with alacrity. 'We shall be leaving shortly. I have an engagement this evening and we must get back. I'm sure that Trottie will go on well, but if you are worried please do not hesitate to let me know. I'll be in touch with Mr Wyatt, who will let you know when she may return home.'

She thanked him, poured the tea and watched the cake she had baked early that morning being demolished. Not a word had been said about their previous meeting. Presumably it wasn't to be referred to again and everything was to be left for Mr Willett to deal with.

They got up to go presently, and Peter asked eagerly if Mr van Linssen would come again soon.

As he always did, Mr van Linssen gave him a serious answer. 'Perhaps not here, Peter. I shall certainly go to the hospital when the time comes, to take off Trottie's plaster and put on a fresh one, and just to make sure that she's as good as new.'

'You wouldn't have time...?'

Eulalia said in a wooden voice, 'Peter, dear, Mr van Linssen's a very busy person. I expect he'll come if he has the time, but his time isn't always his own. He can't do what he likes...'

Mr van Linssen grinned.

Driving back to London, he observed to Dodge, 'Miss Trott is rather a nice person, isn't she?'

'A charming little lady, sir. I must say I was much taken with her. We got on famously.'

A remark which gave his master a good deal of satisfaction. In the intervals of their desultory conversation he bent his powerful brain to set his plans for the future in motion. As they were nearing the end of their journey he said carelessly, 'I may want you to drive down again, take Miss Trott flowers and so on—I can't get away, and if there are any small problems you can let me know.'

'With pleasure, sir.' And Dodge did that rare thing, he smiled.

* * *

Watching the Bentley's tail-lights disappear along the village street, Eulalia reminded herself that allowing Mr van Linssen to occupy her thoughts was a waste of time, and downright dangerous now that she had at last admitted to herself that she liked him after all. Her efforts to forget him were frustrated by Peter, who wished to talk about him at length, and despite herself she found that she was talking about him with as much enthusiasm as Peter.

The next day, however, with Peter at school, she shut him from her mind, although he did have a nasty way of popping back into her thoughts at odd moments. Still, she had a lot to do before she caught the bus to visit Trottie in the afternoon. Peter was to go back with the rector's son until she got home, and Jacob had promised to feed and exercise Charlie and keep an eye on Blossom. The village, sympathetic to a man, were only too willing to help in any way that they could. She shopped quickly, prepared a meal for the evening, packed the things Trottie had asked for and caught the bus to Cirencester.

Trottie looked quite her old self. 'I've been out of bed,' she said proudly. 'Home by the end of the week, Mr Wyatt said. You're managing, Miss Lally?'

Eulalia assured her that she was, handing over the knitting, several magazines, more nighties and the last of the roses from the garden before sitting down to talk.

'That's a nice man, that Mr Dodge,' said Trottie. 'We got on a treat. Fair took to him, I did.'

'He is nice,' agreed Eulalia. 'He and Peter get on famously.'

'He's devoted to Mr van Linssen, thinks the world of him.' She looked at Eulalia over her spectacles. 'Says he works too hard, loves his work.'

Since Eulalia made no reply to this, she began to talk about something else and didn't mention him again. As Eulalia said goodbye she observed, 'Not very happy, are you, Miss Lally? Still bothering about the cottage and the money?'

'No, no, I'm going to see Mr Willett tomorrow and then forget about it.'

'But we can't manage unless you get a job, and I'll not be of much use for a bit.'

'Don't worry about it, Trottie, of course we'll manage, we always have. It'll be lovely to have you back, we do miss you. I'll be in tomorrow about the same time.'

Going back in the bus she pondered the future. She would have to ask Mr Willett to delay the payment of the rent for a few weeks. The money could be paid back at once, the sooner the better, although she would miss it fearfully, and as soon as Trottie could be left alone she would find work in Cirencester or Malmesbury. There was no good in brooding over it.

She showed a cheerful face to Peter when she collected him from the Rectory, and regaled him with a description of her visit to Trottie over their supper. 'I'm going again tomorrow, Peter, but I won't go the next day because it's your half-day from school and I thought we might go and look for cob-nuts.'

She saw Mr Willett the next day and was a little surprised that he agreed readily to return what money remained in the bank. 'As to the rent of the cottage, there is no hurry for that, for Mr van Linssen's solicitor hasn't decided how much it will be. I'll let you know in due course.'

When she saw Trottie she told her that everything had been arranged and there was absolutely no need to think any more about it. 'And I'll not come tomorrow, Trottie, since it's Peter's half-day, but I'll be in the following day.'

When next she saw Trottie she was sitting out of bed, her plastered leg supported on a pillowed stool and a vase of yellow roses on the table beside her. 'Nice, eh?' she wanted to know as Eulalia bent to kiss her. 'That nice Mr Dodge came to see me yesterday, would you believe it? Brought them roses and a great box of chocolates and stayed talking for an hour or more. Said he had a bit of time to himself and fancied a nice drive into the country. We had ever such a nice talk.'

'Trottie, you've got a beau!'

'Go on with you, Miss Lally, and me nigh on sixty. Mr Dodge—he's sixty next month—don't mean to leave Mr van Linssen's service, been with him for years.' Her usually cheerful voice sounded wistful. 'He did say he might pop down again some time—wants to show me an old cookery-book he had from his granny. He still uses the recipes in it.' She added, 'Mr van Linssen's been in Scotland, operating on some bigwig, then he went to Ireland to operate on some poor men who had their kneecaps shot away. He's a dab hand with bones, Mr Dodge said.'

The village rallied round when Trottie came home; the local taxi fetched her and refused to take his fare, the butcher supplied his choicest leg of lamb, the greengrocer carried up a basket of vegetables and the baker offered a cake, and Mr Wedge, not to be outdone, delivered a dozen bottles of milk stout. She held court for several days, sitting in the living-room, and stumped around on her crutches, making sure Eulalia was keeping the kitchen as she liked it. She slept in the dining-room,

for the stairs were beyond her, on a bed Eulalia had bor-
rowed from the Boy and Horseshoe, and life quickly
settled down again. But it wasn't safe to leave her, Eulalia
had decided. She would have to wait until Trottie had
had her plaster changed and was quite confident on her
crutches.

Trottie had been home for two weeks when Mr Dodge
arrived in the Rover. He had brought flowers again and
a basket of fruit, not the apples and pears which were
so easy to come by in the village, but pineapples and
grapes and hot-house peaches. He stayed for tea, and
since he had come soon after lunch Eulalia felt free to
go into Cirencester once more and see Mr Willett. Not
that she got any satisfaction from that gentleman. There
was no news of the rent, she was told, these things took
time. So she went back home and found Trottie and Mr
Dodge in the kitchen making cucumber sandwiches and
toasting tea-cakes. A prosaic occupation and yet she detected a distinct whiff of romance.

It wasn't until he was on the point of going that he
handed Eulalia an envelope. It contained a scrawled note
from Mr van Linssen, informing her that he would be
coming the following morning to take Trottie to the hospital. 'About ten o'clock,' said Dodge, 'if Miss Trott
could be ready by then. I am to say that there will be
no need for you to accompany her and she will be
brought back as soon as possible.'

'Is something wrong?' Eulalia looked anxiously at
Dodge. 'There's nothing in this note...'

'I apprehend that Miss Trott is to be examined to make
sure that the wound on her leg has healed properly.' He

added with an air of reproach, 'Mr van Linssen would have told you if there was anything you should know.'

She agreed meekly.

Mr van Linssen arrived at ten o'clock the next day, pleasantly refused the coffee she offered, and lost no time in packing Trottie neatly into the car. His manner was brisk. Obviously he was a man with no time to waste, although he spared a moment to tumble Charlie and lay a gentle finger on Blossom. Rather daunted by his manner, Eulalia offered lunch on their return. It was refused with polite regret, so that she said with a sudden burst of temper, 'I can't think why you should spend your valuable time driving all this way. We are most grateful, of course, but I can easily hire a car next time.'

He turned at the door as he left the cottage, and gave her a look—it was a look to melt her bones and she took a step backwards, blinded by the sudden shock of it. This was neither the time nor the place in which to fall in love, and if she wasn't careful she would make a fool of herself. It was a mercy that he didn't like her overmuch; everything he had done for them was because he liked Peter...

He got into the car and drove away and she made herself smile and wave to Trottie, wedged into the back seat, but alone in the small sitting-room there was no need to smile. She felt overwhelming relief that she hadn't lost her head and flung herself at him, but he had looked at her...

She must have been mistaken. His manner had been brusque, even if polite. She would need to match her manner with his, and once Trottie was well there would be no need to see him again—she had said that several times already and each time Fate had stepped in.

Anxious to forget her unhappy thoughts, she flung herself into an orgy of housework.

The morning became noon and then afternoon and there was no sign of them. Eulalia ate a sandwich and made a cup of coffee and tidied herself. They would certainly want tea . . .

She was in the kitchen and didn't hear the Bentley's silent stop. They were in the sitting-room before she realised it. She cast a satisfied eye over the scones she had just taken from the oven, switched on the kettle and went to meet them.

Mr van Linssen was helping Trottie off with her coat. 'Everything is exactly as it should be,' he observed. 'In a few weeks the plaster can be changed and in the meantime she may get around on her crutches, as long as she doesn't get tired.'

'That's great. Tea's ready.' Eulalia didn't quite look at him.

'I must leave you to enjoy it. I've an engagement this evening.'

His Ursula, of course. She said brightly, 'Oh, I'm sorry you can't stay. Thank you for coming—it made it so easy for Trottie.'

She saw him to the door, looking no higher than his chin and longing for him to kiss her again. But he didn't. He said nothing at all, shook Trottie's hand and was gone, all within the space of a few minutes.

'I made some scones,' said Eulalia. 'I thought he might have stayed, but of course he wouldn't want to, would he? Not after the fuss about the money and the cottage. Perhaps I should have said something about it . . .'

'Best leave well alone,' said Trottie, 'and I could do with one of those scones, love. I had a nice lunch at the hospital while my plaster was drying. Ever so kind they were, all trooping around behind Mr van Linssen like the stars around the sun. Real famous he is, so one of the nurses told me, travels all over the place putting bones to rights.'

Eulalia listened eagerly. Any crumb of news about him was to be treasured and sorted and stored away. Loving him, she could see, would be a great waste of time but she wasn't sure how to stop it. Perhaps once she had got over the first delicious thrill of it she would be able to damp it down.

She fetched the scones and made the tea and listened to Trottie's account of her day, and presently she went to fetch Peter from the Rectory and the evening's activities swamped any private thoughts.

The weeks went by, enlivened by visits from Dodge, carrying flowers for Trottie and sweets for Peter. They looked forward to seeing him although, to Eulalia's sorrow, he never mentioned Mr van Linssen. It was obvious that he was taken with Trottie and she with him; they went for short, careful walks together and Trottie looked ten years younger. It seemed very likely that they would marry, and Eulalia, while happy to know that her friend's future was secure, wondered how best she could rearrange her own. If and when Trottie married Dodge she would, of course, take her pension with her and there would be no money at all. The problem would be to find work which fitted in with being at home for Peter when he got back from school each day. It would have to fit in with the buses going either to Cirencester or Malmesbury and allow her to be at home when he returned. It was a worry which kept her awake at night, one which she felt she couldn't share with Trottie.

It wasn't until Dodge had driven away on one of the frequent visits that Trottie said, 'Miss Lally, dear, Dodge and me are wishful to marry, but not until the time's right. Dodge will tell Mr van Linssen and bide by what he says.'

Eulalia gave her a hug and wished her happy and said light-heartedly that she and Dodge were made for each other. 'He's a good man, Trottie, and I know you'll be happy. What fun to have a wedding in the family.' Later, though, when Trottie had gone to bed, she sat in the kitchen, staring at the wall, wishing with all her heart that by some mysterious means Fenno van Linssen would come and sort out her life for her.

Had she but known, that was exactly what he was doing. Dodge had apprised him of his wish to marry Trottie and he had expressed pleased surprise, delighted that his attempt to play Cupid had been so successful.

'We would wish to remain in your service, sir,' said Dodge.

'Well, of course—I couldn't manage without you, Dodge, and having Miss Trott is a bonus, isn't it?'

'Certainly it is, sir. But what about Miss Lally?'

'Ah, yes, a matter which must be looked into as soon as possible.'

Dodge went back to his kitchen, leaving Mr van Linssen to sit back in his chair and allow his thoughts to dwell upon Eulalia. A proud piece, he reflected lovingly, who would probably deny her love out of sheer cussedness. It was, he decided, time to do something about that, but first things first.

He had had a long day—six hours in Theatre, a ward round, several private patients to see at the end of the afternoon—nevertheless, that evening he drove to Ursula's home. He should be feeling guilty, he thought, at putting an end to their engagement, but it had weeks ago become a farce. Ursula had relied on her pretty face and amusing manner to attract him, and once they had become engaged she had allowed her selfishness and impatience at his work to take over. He had known for some time that she was marrying him for his money and position and not because she loved him, and he, knowing this, had lost any feeling for her long ago—since, he had to admit, he had walked into the flower shop and seen Eulalia...

The maid answered the door, and when he asked if Miss Kendall was at home she said in a fluster, 'Yes, sir, in the drawing-room, but I don't know...'

He didn't wait to hear the rest of it but went up the staircase two at a time and opened the imposing door. Ursula was there, so was the American he had met at the dinner party. They were so closely locked in each other's arms that neither of them saw Fenno for a few moments.

He didn't say anything, but stood leaning against the door, smiling a little. Kindly Fate was helping his plans along very nicely. It was Ursula who broke the silence. 'So here you are, ready to spend half an hour with me out of your precious day—well, you needn't bother! I've decided not to marry you. I'd die of boredom within a month.' She gave him a defiant look. 'I'm going to marry Wilbur.'

Mr van Linssen strolled across the room. 'We met at a dinner party some weeks ago, did we not?' He shook hands with the man. 'Congratulations, and you, Ursula. I do hope you will be very happy.' He bent and pecked her cheek and she began to tug the ring off her finger. 'No. Oh, no, keep it. What would I want with a diamond ring?' He smiled a little. Eulalia would get his grandmother's old-fashioned sapphire and rose diamond ring, handed down from one bride to the next. He said blandly, 'I won't interrupt your plans for the evening. I'll see myself out.'

He left the house, whistling cheerfully. He wasn't in the least tired and he still had a good deal of planning to do.

CHAPTER NINE

MR DODGE came on the following Friday, but he came in Mr van Linssen's car and Mr van Linssen was driving. Eulalia was in the kitchen baking an apple tart and it was Trottie who stumped to the door on her crutches and let them in.

She lifted her face with the unselfconsciousness of a child for Dodge's kiss, and was kissed in turn by Mr van Linssen. 'She's in the kitchen,' she said. 'Arthur, help me on with my coat. We'll go the the Boy and Horseshoe and get a bottle of sherry. I dare say there'll be coffee by the time we get back.'

Dodge allowed his features to relax into a smile and Mr van Linssen laughed. 'I haven't wished you happy yet. I do with all my heart—Dodge is a lucky man.'

Eulalia had heard their voices, and when he opened the kitchen door she was standing, the rolling-pin in her hand, her face pale, her heart thumping nineteen to the dozen. He closed the door gently behind him and said, 'Hello, Eulalia. Do you intend to whack me with that rolling-pin?'

She was having trouble with her breath. 'No, no. I—I'm surprised. I'm making apple tart—that's all.'

He came up to the table. 'Oh, good, for I have come, so to speak, holding an olive-branch in my hand.'

'An olive-branch?' she repeated stupidly. 'What for?'

'I believe that it is Peter's half-term on Thursday?' When she nodded, he added, 'I'm going to Holland that day—perhaps he might like to come with me, and you too, of course.'

'Go with you? To Holland?' She gathered her scattered wits together. 'We haven't passports.'

'A minor detail. Will you come, Eulalia?' He smiled at her then, and she picked up the rolling-pin again so that she need not look at him.

'We can't—Charlie and Blossom—and I won't leave Trottie alone.'

'Well, of course not. Dodge will come and stay with her and look after things.'

He had an answer for everything.

She tried again, still studying the rolling-pin. 'Miss Kendall—is she going to Holland with you?'

'No, no. I rather think that in the near future she will be going to the States. A most suitable match, I gather, although I deplore his taste in ties.' She raised her eyes long enough to inspect his—Italian silk, richly sombre and probably wildly expensive. He went on in a casual voice, 'We—er—agreed to differ on the subject of marrying.'

'None of this has anything to do with me,' said Eulalia in a high voice.

'Don't be a silly girl. All I am doing is offering Peter and you a few days' holiday. You will stay at my home but I shall be away almost all of the time. Is it not a good opportunity for Dodge and Trottie to get to know each other?' He added in a smug voice, 'We mustn't be selfish.'

She rolled the pastry for an unnecessary length of time. 'Would you take Peter alone? There's really no need for me to go with him.'

'My dear girl, am I expected to see that he changes his socks and washes behind his ears?'

'No. Isn't there another woman there to do that?'

She glanced up and saw his smile. 'Oh, yes, several. You will be quite safe, Eulalia.'

'Well, I'll have to think about it.' She tried to sound cool but her voice wobbled a bit at the thought of spending several days with him.

'By all means,' he agreed affably. 'You can tell me when we've had coffee.'

'I said think about it,' she said crossly, 'and I must ask Peter...'

'Without wishing to state the obvious, I suspect that he will want to go.' He wandered off to meet Trottie and Dodge as they came in, and Eulalia made coffee and found the biscuits, and if she didn't have overmuch to say for herself no one appeared to notice.

Dodge washed the cups and saucers, and she sat uneasily while Trottie and Mr van Linssen discussed the weather. 'It's getting chilly,' he observed. 'Holland always seems colder. Well, it is, of course. You had better bring something warm with you, Eulalia.'

Trottie looked suitably surprised. 'Going on a bit of a holiday, Miss Lally—and Peter too? Do you both good, that peaked you've been looking lately.'

Eulalia shot him a dark look. A mean trick, pinning her down to give an answer with Trottie there. 'I haven't...' she began, and caught his eye. He wasn't smiling but something in his steady look made her pause. She said weakly, powerless, it seemed, to prevent her tongue from uttering the words, 'Yes, we're going on holiday, Trottie—just for a few days—it's Peter's half-term.'

'I dare say Holland's as nice as England,' said Trottie. 'Well, almost. I've not much liking for foreign parts, myself.' She smiled at Mr van Linssen. 'Begging your pardon, though I don't count you as foreign.'

'You flatter me, Trottie. You shall come to Holland with Dodge later. He considers it quite a pleasant place.'

He got to his feet. 'Well, we must go. I'm sorry I can't stop to see Peter, but I've a list at three o'clock. If I'm to take some time off I must work a little harder first. Eulalia, get your passports from the post office—they'll only be temporary but we can get permanent ones later on. I'll be here quite early on Thursday morning and Dodge will be with me.' He bent to kiss Trottie's cheek and made way for Dodge before turning away. 'We shall go from Dover and get home in the late afternoon.'

He gave her an avuncular pat on the shoulder and went out to the car where Dodge joined him. She watched him drive away, torn between a great wish to go with him and annoyance at the high-handed way he had got her to agree to do as he wanted.

Peter, home from school, could hardly contain his excitement. 'Whereabouts in Holland?' he wanted to know.

'I'm not exactly sure...'

'Well, it doesn't really matter, does it? It's abroad, isn't it? Wait till I tell the boys at school. Aunt Lally, I'm so excited.'

Eulalia had to admit that she was excited too.

For the moment, she put aside her problems, fetched the passports, packed clothes for the two of them, and worried about money, which was a bit silly for she had almost none to worry about. In the end she went to Cirencester again and pawned her watch—a gold one her grandmother had given her on her twenty-first birthday.

Thursday came, and with it Mr van Linssen and Dodge. No time was lost; greetings were exchanged, farewells said, Charlie and Blossom embraced for the last time, Eulalia ushered into the back of the car and Peter, to his delight, settled in the front seat. It had all been done, she reflected, without fuss or bustle; she would have encountered far more bustle catching the bus to Cirencester. She supposed that Mr van Linssen travelled so much that a mere trip to Holland was taken in his stride. She sat quietly, half listening to Peter's small voice and Mr van Linssen's deep tones as he drove south.

He broke the journey at a service station, telling them that he would meet them in the café in five minutes' time. Eulalia, hurrying Peter in the direction of the loos, was grateful for his matter-of-factness. They had sandwiches and coffee and got back into the car, Peter clutching a bar of chocolate. 'In case you get peckish,' said Mr van Linssen.

They had travelled on the motorways for almost all the distance, in the fast lane, and as far as Eulalia knew it was motorway until they reached Dover—as it proved to be. The Bentley made nothing of the distance; they were slowing down as they reached the harbour while she was still lost in daydreams.

Once on board they went on deck, so that Peter could watch as the ferry left Dover, and then they went to the restaurant for a meal, and all the while Mr van Linssen kept up a flow of easy talk about nothing in particular, answering Peter's flow of questions with patience, evading her attempts to ask the questions hovering on her tongue. When at last she got her chance he answered casually, 'My home is in a small village close to some lakes, a short distance from Utrecht and Hilversum. We'll drive up the coast into Holland. Once we are over the border it will be motorway again, I'm afraid, but it is the quickest way, and Peter will be needing his supper and bed.'

With that she had to be content.

Once they had landed, he took the road north out of Calais, following the coast into Belgium and to the border town of Sluis. It wasn't a fast road but it was almost free of traffic and, unlike the motorway to Antwerp and beyond, there was plenty to see—small villages, churches and neat villas. She suspected that he had come that way so that Peter wouldn't get bored. Breskens, where they would have to take another ferry, was only a few miles from Sluis and a ferry was waiting. It was a short crossing, but there was time to have a cup of coffee and then go on deck in the chilly evening so that Mr van Linssen could point out exactly where they were. They joined the motorway when they landed at Vlissingen.

'Just over a hundred miles now,' said Mr van Linssen, and joined the stream of traffic. It sounded a long way, but he put his large, well-shod foot down and raced along. Eulalia supposed that there were driving restrictions in Holland as well as in England, although the cars seemed to be going very much faster, perhaps because the country was so flat that one could see ahead for miles—no hedges, no corners, no hills. They were by-passing Breda in forty minutes and turning north to Utrecht. It was dark by the time they got there, but the lights from the city lit up the sky as they passed it, taking the motorway to Amsterdam now. Not for very far, though; he turned the car off the motorway and into a country road. There was a glimmer of water and trees, and presently a village, and few minutes later they were turning in between brick pillars to stop before his home.

'We're here, aren't we?' asked Peter, as Mr van Linssen unbuckled his belt, and he turned round to say, 'Aunt Lally, I'm so excited, aren't you?'

Of course she was; she was scared too. What on earth had she been thinking of to come all this way, meet any number of people she didn't know and who might not like her or Peter? Who were the people, anyway? She knew absolutely nothing about him or his home. She got out of the car when he opened the door for her, feeling a little mad. The sight of the house didn't reassure her either. It stood for so much: wealth and gracious living and a proud ancestry. No wonder he was so arrogant. No, not arrogant, just sure of himself...

The door had been opened, allowing light to stream out, and a grey-haired man came down the steps to meet them.

'Pete.' Mr van Linssen shook his hand. 'Eulalia, Peter, this is Pete, who runs this place with his wife Anneke. Pete, Miss Warburton and Peter.'

They shook hands and Pete said, 'A pleasure to meet you, miss, and Peter.'

Eulalia said quickly, 'Oh, you speak English. Peter and I can't speak Dutch, I'm afraid.'

'No worry, miss. Anneke speaks only Dutch, but I will be there too.'

They were inside the house by now and Anneke came to meet them, to be greeted with a hug by Mr van Linssen before they were introduced once more. He said something to the housekeeper, who took their coats while Pete fetched the luggage and Mr van Linssen said briskly, 'Let us find my mother. She will be expecting us.'

'Your mother?'

He took her arm. 'Did I not mention her? She stays here frequently, although she lives in den Haag. She will be in the drawing-room, I expect.'

He opened the double doors and ushered them inside. The room was magnificent—high-ceilinged, its walls hung with mulberry-red silk. There were high-backed armchairs on either side of the blazing fire in the great stone hearth, and a wide sofa, backed by a sofa table, facing it. Great bow-fronted cabinets stood against two walls and a brass *stoelklok* with its ponderous slow tick-tock hung between the long windows. There was a chandelier hanging from the ceiling, a glistening crystal waterfall, but it wasn't lighted; a number of small lamps stood around on the small tables set here and there around the room, casting a gentle glow, and there were ormulu wall-lights.

Eulalia heard Peter's gasp as they went forward to meet the elderly lady getting out of her chair. She was tall, as tall and as big as Eulalia, and still a good-looking woman. Her hair was grey and severely dressed and her eyes were as blue as her son's, and she was smiling.

'Fenno, you're here at last.' She lifted her face for his kiss. 'And this is Eulalia and Peter.' She offered a hand, adding, 'I may call you Eulalia? You do not mind? It is delightful to have you to stay. You shall tell me all the news from England, and I am looking forward to hearing about Peter's school.'

Mr van Linssen had gone to the French windows at the end of the room and opened them, and a large dog ambled in, to fall all over her master with delight, giving happy yelps. 'Come and meet Sally, Peter. She looks fierce but she's very friendly.'

She was a Bouvier, with a grey woolly coat, small yellow eyes and enormous teeth, a formidable beast if crossed, but just now grinning with pleasure and submitting to Peter's small hands. 'You like dogs?' asked Mevrouw van Linssen of Eulalia.

'Yes. Mr van Linssen gave Peter a puppy; we call him Charlie...'

Mevrouw van Linssen took her arm. 'You will want to go to your room and tidy yourself, my dear. Anneke shall take you and Peter upstairs, but don't be long, for we shall dine early so that Peter can go to bed.'

Anneke came then and clucked in a motherly fashion over Peter and led them across the hall to the staircase curving against one wall to the gallery above. It was a rather grand staircase with carved banisters, and the wooden treads were worn by generations of feet.

They had rooms side by side with a shared bathroom, and the moment Anneke left them Peter said in an awed whisper, 'Aunt Lally, it's very grand, like a palace. Mr van Linssen must have lots of money. I wonder why he works when he doesn't need to?'

'I think because he likes being a surgeon, dear.'

Peter nodded and said, 'Yes, I expect so.'

They explored their rooms together, charmed by the narrow canopied beds hung with muslin curtains, and their coverlets of toile de Jouy, the matching curtains and the William and Mary marquetry chests. In Peter's room there was a tulip-wood dressing-table on delicate castors and a small tub armchair, just right for his size. There were books too—children's books on the small

table by the bed. Someone had gone to a great deal of
trouble, thought Eulalia, inspecting in her turn her own
room, with its Georgian dressing-table set between the
two windows, a Dutch marquetry toilet mirror on it.
There was a cheval-glass in one corner of the room too,
and she took a quick look at her person. Her plain wool
dress couldn't compete with her hostess's elegant outfit,
but it would pass muster. She went into Peter's room,
made sure that he had washed his face and hands,
brushed his hair and went downstairs again.

There was sherry in the drawing-room and lemonade
for Peter and ten minutes' pleasant talk before they
crossed the hall to the dining-room. It was not as large
as the drawing-room but equally grand, with a massive
sideboard and an oval table which could seat a dozen
without difficulty. They sat at one end of it, Mr van
Linssen at the head, his mother on his right and Eulalia,
with Peter beside her, on his left, while Pete served them
with soup, chicken in a delicious sauce and a chocolate
pudding rich with cream. They drank a white wine and
Pete poured apple-juice for Peter.

Mr van Linssen was a splendid host, maintaining a
gentle flow of talk which required no effort to answer,
and talking to Peter too, keeping to general topics with
his mother but never once giving a clue about his family
or his life in Holland. Presently, waiting as Peter bade
them goodnight, Eulalia was aware that he was watching
her, but she looked away quickly, afraid that he might
see how happy she was to be there, in his home with
him.

He opened the door as they reached it and touched
her on the arm. 'Come down again, Eulalia.'

She nodded at his waistcoat, very conscious of his hand.

Back in the drawing-room, once Peter had fallen asleep, she sat beside Mevrouw van Linssen on the sofa a little away from him in his armchair, while he suggested how she and Peter might spend their days. He sounded matter-of-fact and friendly. 'I don't need to go to Amsterdam until the afternoon. I thought we might go round the gardens and explore the house. I know Mother will love to gossip after I've gone.'

'Are you staying in Amsterdam?'

'No, no, but I shall be back very late, and I go to Utrecht on the following day and on to Leiden, but I should be home in the early evening. I wondered if you would like to come with me? Utrecht is worth a visit, and so is Leiden. I'll take you both to lunch and then drive to Leiden. I only need to be there for a couple of hours and, if you would like, I'll get someone to take you both round the hospital.'

'That would be marvellous. Peter will be thrilled. Won't we be a nuisance?'

'No, not at all. I'm afraid it is a very small glimpse of Holland.'

'But it's a start,' observed his mother. 'Leiden is a charming little city. I'm sure you'll enjoy it. And I'm looking forward to showing you the village, and we can walk to the lake...'

Eulalia said her goodnights presently and said, 'Please don't get up,' when Mr van Linssen walked to the door with her.

He took no notice at all, but with his hand on the door said, 'I think that you might try and call me Fenno, don't you? After all, we are old acquaintances.' He bent swiftly and kissed her. 'Goodnight, Eulalia.'

She wouldn't sleep, she fretted as she got ready for bed. He shouldn't have kissed her—it wasn't fair, with the business of the cottage and the money still a bone of contention between them—well, on her side at any rate, since he persisted in doing nothing about it or even mentioning it.

She got into bed, ready to lie and worry, but instead went to sleep at once.

The next day was over too soon. They spent the morning roaming round the gardens: acres and acres of lawns, rose-garden and a herb-garden, a walled kitchen-garden, a pond with carp, a gazebo, long walks bordered by herbaceous plants, lying dormant, and a vast greenhouse. Peter, with Sally beside him, ran ahead while Eulalia, quite forgetting her worries, stopped to peer and admire and ask questions.

'However many gardeners do you have, Mr van—— I mean, Fenno?'

'Two, and a boy.' He tucked her hand in his. 'You aren't cold?'

'No, it's lovely, so different...'

'Very quiet, although we are very close to the motorway. You like a country life, don't you, Eulalia?'

She nodded. 'Yes. What's through that little door?'

'A paddock, with stables at the far end housing a pony, a chestnut mare and a donkey.'

Peter would have stayed there for hours, feeding them the carrots and sugar Fenno had brought with him, but they prised him away at last and went indoors to have coffee before looking round the house.

'There won't be time to see all of it. Mother will be delighted to take you round the old wing and the attics.' He took her hand and they went upstairs with Peter and Sally to begin their tour. There were several doors round the gallery and passages to the left and right, as well as half a dozen stairs leading to the back of the house. They went from room to room, each one perfect, until he glanced at his watch.

'I have to go—there's one more room I want to show you.'

He led the way to the front of the gallery and opened a double door. The room overlooked the front gardens, its three tall windows draped in pastel brocade, the bed a vast four-poster with curtains of the same brocade. There were tallboys and a vast chest against one wall, and a dressing-table with a triple mirror and a low stool, and all of them were in tulip-wood and marquetry. There were comfortable chairs too, and a day-bed at the foot of the four-poster.

Peter stared round him. 'It's like a room for the Queen.'

Mr van Linssen nodded gravely, his eyes on Eulalia.

He left soon after and they sat down to lunch with Mevrouw van Linssen, and afterwards walked to the village and took a look at the lake. Sally pranced along beside them and Peter ran to and fro, completely happy.

Eulalia, lying in her bed later that night, reflected that it had been a lovely day. Pete had taken Peter to the kitchen to watch Anneke cook, and she and Mevrouw van Linssen had toured the rest of the house—the old wing, seldom used now, a mass of small panelled rooms and narrow passages, and then the attic floor. Not really attics, for they had been made into a flat for Pete and

Anneke and bed-sitting rooms for the two housemaids. Only the vast one over the wing was filled with a hotch-potch of discarded furniture, great cabin-trunks, and a cupboard filled with old-fashioned dresses and hats. They had poked around together while Mevrouw van Linssen chatted of this and that, slipping in a few questions from time to time, so unobtrusively that Eulalia hadn't noticed.

The one flaw in a perfect day had been the lack of Fenno, but tomorrow, she told herself, she would be with him all day.

She woke early, as did Peter, and together they went to look out of the window. It was a fine day but there was a wind, and clouds piling up on the horizon, and striding away down the drive was Fenno with Sally.

'I'd have gone with him if he had asked me,' said Peter.

Me too, thought Eulalia, and urged him to get dressed so that they would be downstairs when he came back.

He wished them a cheerful good morning, remarked that there was a cold wind and that they had better wear something warm, and, once breakfast was eaten, warned them that he wanted to leave in ten minutes.

'You're sure you don't mind?' asked Eulalia, already halfway to the door. 'Taking us, I mean...'

'I'm delighted to have your company, but don't keep me waiting.'

He drove them to a quiet street next to the cathedral in Utrecht, explained how they might reach the shopping streets, and warned them to be back at that spot in three hours' time. 'And don't try and climb the Dom tower, there are four hundred and sixty-five steps. Have you money with you?' He didn't look at her. 'You've had no time to get *guldens*, have you?' He fished in his pocket and handed her some notes, and seeing her attempt to refuse said, 'Don't be silly, you can pay me back later on. We'll have a quick lunch together, but you'll need coffee.'

He got back into the car and drove away. 'I should have liked to have gone with him,' said Peter.

And so, reflected Eulalia, would I.

They spent a long time in the cathedral, took a look at the Dom tower, then found their way to the shops and a café where they had coffee and a milkshake and, since she might as well use the money now that she had it, some luscious cream cakes. They were in a quiet corner, and she opened her purse and counted the *guldens*. More than five hundred—however did he think she could repay him if she were to spend them? She prudently put almost all of it with her sparse bundle of five-pound notes and calculated how much she could afford to borrow. That done to her satisfaction, they went shopping for presents for Trottie and Dodge—a cup and saucer for each of them in Delft blue, not the genuine china but pretty, nevertheless, and by then it was time to find their way back to the little side-street again, pausing to hang over the little arched bridges and watch the boats on the canals and gaze up at the old gabled houses.

The Bentley nosed its way round the corner as they turned into the street. 'Enjoyed your morning?' Fenno wanted to know. 'We'll have lunch and drive on to Leiden.'

He took them to the Café de Paris, smart and expensive, with a décor which left Peter's eyes wide open.

'Something quick,' he suggested.

'Whatever you suggest...'

'Omelettes? And french fries for Peter?' He gave the order and asked for coffee at the same time, and an orange drink for Peter, who plied him with questions about the hospital until a plate was set before him and he began on the french fries. It was a pleasant meal, even if they wasted no time over it; indeed, Peter was finished first, impatient to be gone since they were to go round the hospital in Leiden.

It was thirty miles to Leiden, a distance the Bentley covered in less than half an hour, and Mr van Linssen drove straight to the hospital. 'I shall be here for an hour or so—why not walk a little way along Rapenburg by the canal, and come back here in about half an hour? I'll leave word at the lodge. Just say who you are.'

So they walked a bit, and discovered the university and the Hortus Botanicus gardens, the library and a museum, and presently presented themselves at the porter's lodge and were handed over to a young doctor.

'Wim Bakker,' he introduced himself. 'Mr van Linssen asked me to show you round.'

'How kind, but shouldn't you be working?' Eulalia liked him at once.

'I have a few hours off duty.' His English was as good as hers.

'Then we're taking up your precious free time.'

'It is a pleasure, Miss Warburton.' He smiled down at Peter. 'You wish to be a great man like our Mr van Linssen? And why not? Let us start our tour.'

They were in the entrance hall an hour or so later when Mr van Linssen joined them, asked if they had enjoyed themselves, thanked Wim and swept them out to the car, his manner a mixture of the avuncular and the impatient, at least with Eulalia; with Peter he was painstakingly kind, answering questions and explaining things.

It was the same when they returned to his home, so that she became stiff and shy with him; she had been a fool in rose-coloured spectacles just because he had invited her and Peter for a few days' holiday and had broken off his engagement to Ursula. She went hot and cold at the thought that she had given herself away, and that evening, after Peter was in bed and they were sitting in the drawing-room, when Mevrouw van Linssen remarked that she and Peter had had a very full day, and Fenno capped that by observing that she must be tired, she seized on it as an excuse to take herself off to bed, where she wept herself to sleep.

They left for England the next morning. Mevrouw van Linssen kissed her warmly with the remark that a longer stay would have been very pleasant. 'But of course, Peter mustn't miss his schooling, must he?' she said, and waved them away cheerfully. She lifted her face for her son's kiss and said that she expected to see him again. 'Very soon,' she added with a wide smile.

The journey home was made with the ease Eulalia was beginning to expect from Fenno, with just enough time when they reached Calais to go on board and a quick getaway when they reached Dover. He stopped at a service station so that Peter might have egg and chips while he and Eulalia had coffee and sandwiches, and when they were once more on their way he delighted Peter by phoning Dodge from the car to let him know that they would be home in time for supper. He and Peter kept up a seemingly endless conversation for most of the journey, casting an occasional remark over their shoulders to her, so that she had all the time in the world to think. Not that she solved any of her problems.

They arrived at Ivy Cottage to a warm welcome and a pleasant flurry of activity from Dodge and Trottie, and they sat down to supper almost at once. Between them they had produced a meal fit for a king: prawn cocktails, minute steaks with creamed potatoes and baby sprouts, and one of Trottie's apple pies for afters, and, since Trottie was full of questions, Eulalia forgot her problems for the moment, thinking how delightful it was, all of them sitting round the table with Charlie and Blossom pacing to and fro in the hope of titbits, and of course Fenno sitting at its head.

She was taken quite by surprise when the meal had been cleared and Fenno said casually, 'Well, we must be off. You're ready, Dodge?'

'Off?' said Eulalia. 'You're going back to London now?'

'Like Peter, I have to work tomorrow.'

Trottie and Dodge were in the kitchen but Peter was standing by Fenno, so even if she had wanted to, there was no chance to say anything. What would she say, anyway? she wondered forlornly, as she expressed her thanks with suitable politeness.

'I'm glad you enjoyed your visit. Far too brief, though. We must do better next time.'

'There won't be a next time,' she said very fast, quite forgetting Peter.

'But, Aunt Lally, why can't we go again? I liked it, and I like being with Mr van Linssen.'

'He's a busy man, Peter. I'm sure he has very little time for—for...'

'His friends?' asked Fenno blandly. 'For those he loves? You are mistaken, Eulalia. He has all the time in the world.'

She didn't look at him, and Peter, happy again, went out to the car with him, and Dodge wished her goodbye and got in beside his master. The car was out of sight when she realised that Fenno hadn't said goodbye. She supposed that she had deserved that.

With Peter back at school, she picked up the threads of her life once more. The future was precarious and first she must talk to Trottie. That lady, when asked when she was going to marry, parried the question with a vague, 'Well, Miss Lally, it all depends...'

'On what, Trottie?'

'One thing and another. I'm not going up the aisle with my leg in a plaster, that's for sure.' Trottie looked up from the table where she was polishing glasses. 'And that reminds me, I'm to have another plaster on Friday. Mr van Linssen told Dodge he could take the Rover and fetch me. Such a kind man. Dodge'll be here around nine o'clock. You'll be all right on your own?'

'Of course.' Eulalia made her voice sound cheerful; after all, before long she would be on her own, wouldn't she? And Trottie, dear Trottie, who had shared everything with her without complaint, must marry just as soon as possible. It would be a good opportunity while she was at the hospital to collect as many newspapers as possible and look for part-time work. She knew to a penny how much she needed to keep Peter and herself, and there were one or two things she could sell. His school trust, thank heaven, was more than enough for the fees, so she could fit him out as he grew. She would manage. She asked, 'Are you going to live at Mr van Linssen's house when you are married? It's very nice there, not a bit like Cromwell Road. You'll like it.'

'Well, we'll wait and see,' said Trottie, infuriatingly refusing to give a plain answer.

It was hard to maintain a cheerful face, since Peter talked about Mr van Linssen incessantly and it seemed to her that Trottie encouraged him. If only she could go somewhere and have a good cry about it and then forget him.

Friday came and with it Dodge, driving sedately down the village street. He wished Eulalia a dignified good morning, when she wasn't looking kissed Trottie, and then helped her carefully into the car and drove away. They might not be back until the afternoon, he observed, and if Trottie was tired he hoped that Eulalia wouldn't object if he took her for some refreshment.

'Heavens, of course I don't mind, Dodge. Have a nice lunch or something—there are lots of good restaurants in Cirencester—and come back when you like. I'm going into the village now but I'll be in for the rest of the day.'

The moment the car was out of sight she got into her coat and hurried to the newsagent in the main street, where she bought every likely paper as well as *The Lady* magazine, and bore them back, and with Blossom on her lap and Charlie beside her, she spread them out on the kitchen table and began looking for work.

There weren't many jobs which she could do. Checkout at a supermarket, someone to deliver circulars in Malmesbury, someone to look after a frail elderly lady, hours to suit—she wondered what that meant, to suit her or the old lady? Someone to walk two dogs twice a day, a young lady to demonstrate a new brand of margarine at one of the supermarkets. She made a list and then, surrounded by newspapers, she composed a letter applying for each of them. A job, any job, was necessary, so that Trottie would feel free to go. With luck, she reflected, she might be able to fit in two part-time jobs, as long as they were both in Cirencester...

She was on her third attempt at an application when the knocker was thumped, and before she could get up the door was thrown open and Fenno came in.

'Well, really,' said Eulalia, short of breath and with her heart thumping against her ribs, torn between surprise and delight and rage. 'How did you get here?' she managed, as he closed the door behind him and locked it, put the key on the table and picked up her last effort.

He looked at her over the top of it. 'In my car. Although if it had been necessary I would have walked.'

'Walked all the way from London? Why?'

He fended off Charlie with a gentle hand. 'Because I wanted to see you and, come to that, I would walk from the other side of the world if I had to. Even though I would not be sure of my reception, for a more obstinate, pig-headed girl I have yet to meet!' He swept the newspapers off the table and pulled her gently into his arms, ignoring her indignant gasp. 'I took you to Holland because I had a sentimental wish to ask you to marry me while we were in my home, but you were so polite and distant. Why?'

She stared at his waistcoat buttons. 'I thought... Well, I'd only just discovered... What I mean is...'

Mr van Linssen considered this a sufficiently satisfactory answer to allow him to tighten his hold and kiss her soundly.

'I'm not pig-headed,' said Eulalia, 'or obstinate.'

He kissed her again lingeringly. 'You're both, my darling heart. Will you say yes if I ask you to marry me?'

'Yes,' said Eulalia. 'Am I really your darling heart, Fenno?'

'Forever and always, my dear love.'

'Is that why you bought this cottage and gave me all that money?'

'That is why.'

She smiled up at him, and Mr van Linssen, a man of flesh and blood, kissed her again, taking his time.

Harlequin Romance

is proud to announce the latest arrivals in our bouncing baby series

Each month in 1997 we'll be bringing you your very own bundle of joy—a cute, delightful romance by one of your favorite authors. Our heroes and heroines are about to discover that two's company and three (or four...or five) is a family!

Find out about the true labor of love...

Don't miss these charming stories of parenthood, and how to survive it, coming in May, June and July.

**May—THE SECRET BABY (#3457)
by Day Leclaire
June—FOR BABY'S SAKE (#3461)
by Val Daniels
July—BABY, YOU'RE MINE! (#3463)
by Leigh Michaels**

Available wherever Harlequin books are sold.

MILLION DOLLAR SWEEPSTAKES
OFFICIAL RULES
NO PURCHASE NECESSARY TO ENTER

1. To enter, follow the directions published. Method of entry may vary. For eligibility, entries must be received no later than March 31, 1998. No liability is assumed for printing errors, lost, late, non-delivered or misdirected entries.

   To determine winners, the sweepstakes numbers assigned to submitted entries will be compared against a list of randomly, preselected prize winning numbers. In the event all prizes are not claimed via the return of prize winning numbers, random drawings will be held from among all other entries received to award unclaimed prizes.

2. Prize winners will be determined no later than June 30, 1998. Selection of winning numbers and random drawings are under the supervision of D. L. Blair, Inc., an independent judging organization whose decisions are final. Limit: one prize to a family or organization. No substitution will be made for any prize, except as offered. Taxes and duties on all prizes are the sole responsibility of winners. Winners will be notified by mail. Odds of winning are determined by the number of eligible entries distributed and received.

3. Sweepstakes open to residents of the U.S. (except Puerto Rico), Canada and Europe who are 18 years of age or older, except employees and immediate family members of Torstar Corp., D. L. Blair, Inc., their affiliates, subsidiaries, and all other agencies, entities, and persons connected with the use, marketing or conduct of this sweepstakes. All applicable laws and regulations apply. Sweepstakes offer void wherever prohibited by law. Any litigation within the province of Quebec respecting the conduct and awarding of a prize in this sweepstakes must be submitted to the Régie des alcools, des courses et des jeux. In order to win a prize, residents of Canada will be required to correctly answer a time-limited arithmetical skill-testing question to be administered by mail.

4. Winners of major prizes (Grand through Fourth) will be obligated to sign and return an Affidavit of Eligibility and Release of Liability within 30 days of notification. In the event of non-compliance within this time period or if a prize is returned as undeliverable, D. L. Blair, Inc. may at its sole discretion, award that prize to an alternate winner. By acceptance of their prize, winners consent to use of their names, photographs or other likeness for purposes of advertising, trade and promotion on behalf of Torstar Corp., its affiliates and subsidiaries, without further compensation unless prohibited by law. Torstar Corp. and D. L. Blair, Inc., their affiliates and subsidiaries are not responsible for errors in printing of sweepstakes and prize winning numbers. In the event a duplication of a prize winning number occurs, a random drawing will be held from among all entries received with that prize winning number to award that prize.

5. This sweepstakes is presented by Torstar Corp., its subsidiaries and affiliates in conjunction with book, merchandise and/or product offerings. The number of prizes to be awarded and their value are as follows: Grand Prize — $1,000,000 (payable at $33,333.33 a year for 30 years); First Prize — $50,000; Second Prize — $10,000; Third Prize — $5,000; 3 Fourth Prizes — $1,000 each; 10 Fifth Prizes — $250 each; 1,000 Sixth Prizes — $10 each. Values of all prizes are in U.S. currency. Prizes in each level will be presented in different creative executions, including various currencies, vehicles, merchandise and travel. Any presentation of a prize level in a currency other than U.S. currency represents an approximate equivalent to the U.S. currency prize for that level, at that time. Prize winners will have the opportunity of selecting any prize offered for that level; however, the actual non U.S. currency equivalent prize if offered and selected, shall be awarded at the exchange rate existing at 3:00 P.M. New York time on March 31, 1998. A travel prize option, if offered and selected by winner, must be completed within 12 months of selection and is subject to: traveling companion(s) completing and returning of a Release of Liability prior to travel; and hotel and flight accommodations availability. For a current list of all prize options offered within prize levels, send a self-addressed, stamped envelope (WA residents need not affix postage) to: MILLION DOLLAR SWEEPSTAKES Prize Options, P.O. Box 4456, Blair, NE 68009-4456, USA.

6. For a list of prize winners (available after July 31, 1998) send a separate, stamped, self-addressed envelope to: MILLION DOLLAR SWEEPSTAKES Winners, P.O. Box 4459, Blair, NE 68009-4459, USA.

As Seen on TV!

Free Gift Offer

With a Free Gift proof-of-purchase
from any Harlequin® book, you can receive
a beautiful cubic zirconia pendant.

This stunning marquise-shaped stone is a genuine cubic
zirconia—accented by an 18" gold tone necklace.
(Approximate retail value $19.95)

Send for yours today...
compliments of ◆HARLEQUIN®

To receive your free gift, a cubic zirconia pendant, send us one original proof-of-purchase, photocopies not accepted, from the back of any Harlequin Romance®, Harlequin Presents®, Harlequin Temptation®, Harlequin Superromance®, Harlequin Intrigue®, Harlequin American Romance®, or Harlequin Historicals® title available in February, March or April at your favorite retail outlet, together with the Free Gift Certificate, plus a check or money order for $1.65 u.s./$2.15 can. (do not send cash) to cover postage and handling, payable to Harlequin Free Gift Offer. We will send you the specified gift. Allow 6 to 8 weeks for delivery. Offer good until April 30, 1997, or while quantities last. Offer valid in the U.S. and Canada only.

Free Gift Certificate

Name: _____

Address: _____

City: _____ State/Province: _____ Zip/Postal Code: _____

Mail this certificate, one proof-of-purchase and a check or money order for postage and handling to: HARLEQUIN FREE GIFT OFFER 1997. In the U.S.: 3010 Walden Avenue, P.O. Box 9071, Buffalo NY 14269-9057. In Canada: P.O. Box 604, Fort Erie, Ontario L2Z 5X3.

FREE GIFT OFFER   084-KEZ

ONE PROOF-OF-PURCHASE
To collect your fabulous FREE GIFT, a cubic zirconia pendant, you must include this
original proof-of-purchase for each gift with the properly completed Free Gift Certificate.

084-KEZ

HARLEQUIN ROMANCE'S 40TH ANNIVERSARY SWEEPSTAKES
OFFICIAL RULES—NO PURCHASE NECESSARY

To enter, complete an Official Entry Form or 3" x 5" card by hand printing the words "Harlequin Romance's 40th Anniversary Sweepstakes," your name and address thereon and mailing it to: In the U.S., Harlequin Romance's 40th Anniversary Sweepstakes, P.O. Box 9076, Buffalo, NY 14269-9076, or in Canada to Harlequin Romance's 40th Anniversary Sweepstakes, P.O. Box 637, Fort Erie, Ontario L2A 5X3. Limit: one entry per envelope, one prize to an individual, family or organization. Entries must be sent via first-class mail and be received no later than 7/31/97. No liability is assumed for lost, late or misdirected mail.

Prizes: 150 autographed hardbound books (value $9.95 each U.S./$11.98 each CAN.). Winners will be selected in a random drawing (to be conducted no later than 8/29/97) from among all eligible entries received by D. L. Blair, Inc., an independent judging organization whose decisions are final.

IF YOU HAVE INCLUDED THREE HARLEQUIN PROOFS OF PURCHASE PLUS APPROPRIATE SHIPPING AND HANDLING ($1.99 U.S. OR $2.99 CAN.) WITH YOUR ENTRY, YOU WILL RECEIVE A NONAUTOGRAPHED 40TH ANNIVERSARY COLLECTOR'S EDITION BOOK.

Sweepstakes offer is open only to residents of the U.S. (except Puerto Rico) and Canada who are 18 years of age or older, except employees and immediate family members of Harlequin Enterprises, Ltd., their affiliates, subsidiaries, and all other agencies, entities and persons connected with the use, marketing or conduct of this sweepstakes. All federal, state, provincial, municipal and local laws apply. Offer void wherever prohibited by law. Taxes and/or duties on prizes are the sole responsibility of the winners. Any litigation within the province of Quebec respecting the conduct and awarding of a prize in this sweepstakes may be submitted to the Régie des alcools, des courses et des jeux. All prizes will be awarded; winners will be notified by mail. No substitution for prizes is permitted. Odds of winning are dependent upon the number of eligible entries received.

Any prize or prize notification returned as undeliverable may result in the awarding of that prize to an alternative winner. By acceptance of their prize, winners consent to use of their names, photographs or likenesses for purposes of advertising, trade and promotion on behalf of Harlequin Enterprises, Ltd., without further compensation unless prohibited by law. In order to win a prize, residents of Canada will be required to correctly answer a time-limited, arithmetical skill-testing question administered by mail.

For a list of winners (available after September 30, 1997) send a separate stamped, self-addressed envelope to: Harlequin Romance's 40th Anniversary Sweepstakes Winners, P.O. Box 4200, Blair, NE 68009-4200, U.S.A.

Happy Birthday to

Harlequin Romance®

With the purchase of three Harlequin Romance books, you can send in for a **FREE** hardbound collector's edition and automatically enter Harlequin Romance's 40th Anniversary Sweepstakes.

FREE COLLECTOR'S EDITION BOOK

On the official entry form/proof-of-purchase coupon below, fill in your name, address and zip or postal code, and send it, plus $1.99 U.S./$2.99 CAN. for postage and handling (check or money order—please do not send cash), payable to Harlequin Books, to: In the U.S.: 3010 Walden Avenue, P.O. Box 9071, Buffalo, N.Y. 14269-9071; In Canada: P.O. Box 622, Fort Erie, Ontario L2A 5X3. Please allow 4-6 weeks for delivery. Order your **FREE** Collector's Edition now; quantities are limited. Offer for the free hardbound book expires December 31, 1997. Entries for the Specially Autographed 40th Anniversary Collector's Edition draw will be accepted only until July 31, 1997.

WIN A SPECIALLY AUTOGRAPHED
COLLECTOR'S EDITION BOOK

To enter Harlequin Romance's 40th Anniversary Sweepstakes only, hand print on a 3" x 5" card the words "Harlequin Romance's 40th Anniversary Sweepstakes," your name and address and mail to: "40th Anniversary Harlequin Romance Sweepstakes"—in the U.S., 3010 Walden Avenue, P.O. Box 9076, Buffalo, N.Y. 14269-9076; in Canada, P.O. Box 637, Fort Erie, Ontario L2A 5X3. No purchase or obligation necessary to enter. Limit: one entry per envelope. Entries must be sent via first-class mail and be received no later than July 31, 1997. See back-page ad for complete sweepstakes rules.

✂

Happy Birthday, Harlequin Romance!

Official Entry Form/Proof of Purchase

"Please send me my **FREE**
40th Anniversary Collector's Edition book and enter me in
Harlequin Romance's 40th Anniversary Sweepstakes."

Name: _____

Address: _____

City: _____

State/Prov.: _____ Zip/Postal Code: _____

089-KEP

089-KEP